DATE DUE

A FLAT TYRE IN FULHAM

A wages snatch had unexpectedly failed in south London. The discovery of a man's body in the boot of the stolen Jaguar had been a shock. These incidents and the death by drugs and drowning of a teenage prostitute had to be investigated as a matter of urgency.

Scotland Yard police manage to uncover a great deal and the action builds again towards the end of this mystery.

A FLAT TYRE IN FULHAM

Josephine Bell

· BLACK ·
DAGGER
· CRIME ·

First published 1963
by
Hodder & Stoughton Ltd

This edition 2001 by Chivers Press
published by arrangement with
the author's estate

ISBN 0 7540 8579 1

British Library Cataloguing in Publication Data available

Printed and bound in Great Britain by
Redwood Books, Trowbridge, Wiltshire

CHAPTER ONE

THE elegant dark green Jaguar car left the exit from London Airport and swung into the traffic, heading east.

It was not one of the latest models, but a well-kept specimen about four years old. It purred along, passing effortlessly the other cars, vans and lorries on the wide road, sweeping along the Chiswick flyover, slackening speed a little as the traffic thickened on the dual carriageway approaching Hammersmith.

The man at the wheel had been tense at first, concentrating on his driving, looking frequently in his back mirror. But as he neared Hammersmith he relaxed and even went through the complicated process of lighting a cigarette for himself without stopping. He managed this with a skill born of long practice. It was the last one in the packet, but he put the crumpled cardboard in his jacket pocket and the lighter too and pulled out the car's ashtray on the dashboard to a convenient angle.

The morning rush-hour was in full swing. It was astonishing how it piled up in a matter of fifteen minutes, as if all the cars had been arranged and started at their homes on a handicap system and the tape lay in central London, whither they were now all crowding and pushing in barely controlled anarchy.

The solitary driver of the Jaguar paid little attention to this. He drove on, maintaining his evident skill, using his long experience. He drew steadily on the cigarette in his mouth, seeming to depend on it to soothe his temper and render him impervious to the aggressions of the other drivers when they swung across his bows or braked suddenly dead ahead or blared their horns at him. He took every kind of evading action, but he did not lose a yard in doing so.

He drove across the flyover at Hammersmith, thankful as always for the time saved by it; he followed the extension of the Cromwell Road, then the Cromwell Road itself, keeping in the offside lane now to make a turn to the right just before Gloucester Road. The side street was beginning to fill with cars, parked or parking. This delayed him again, but he reached the Old Brompton Road, turned east into it and left it again at Drayton Gardens.

Again he was held up by cars moving into position along the kerbs on each side of the road. He looked at his watch, matching it with the clock on the dashboard. They were out by only two minutes and he still had time to spare. But not much. He pressed on to the Fulham Road, crossed it at the lights and increased speed when he found the street ahead reasonably empty. Five minutes to cross the river, ten to approach. Deadline in fifteen. O.K. He had it in hand.

He pulled out to pass a stationary milk cart. The wheel was suddenly as heavy as lead in his hands. When he pulled in again to his near side he felt the whole car sway and slide.

He knew what had happened. As he slowed down and even before he turned off into a street on his left he heard the ominous bumping of the flat tyre. A flat tyre. In a car of this type. At such a moment. Incredible. But true.

His immediate impulse was to jump out and run, but he controlled himself with a great effort. Fortunately it was still early, only a little after half past nine. There were very few people about, none in the street where he now was.

He dropped the butt of the cigarette as he opened the car door; it dropped on to the floor of the car. He grabbed at the packet in his pocket, remembered it was empty and flung it down, too. Then he got out, taking the ignition key with him. He locked the car, glanced up and down the road and walked away. But he did not glance at the house before whose door he had parked the Jaguar. The woman who had heard him arrive and gone to look through the net curtains, saw the flat front tyre and watched him go. She was vaguely surprised that he had not gone round to look at the puncture, but she concluded that he had gone off to get help. It was what she would do in any crisis. It did not seem strange to her that he made no attempt to repair the damage himself.

The man walked quickly towards the King's Road. The first thing was to find a public telephone. He had about five minutes, that spare five minutes, in which to report what had happened and alter the time-table. If it could be altered.

When he got to the call box it was occupied and his heart sank. But the caller had nearly finished. The delay there was less than a minute. He got through and explained.

'*Burst tyre!*' He heard the fierce emphasis on the words and smiled grimly at the following curses.

'You heard! Not my fault, was it? You can shut your ruddy trap or find another stooge.'

He was taking the receiver from his ear as he spoke, but was checked by a quieter, more authoritative voice at the other end.

'Pipe down!'

'*Me* pipe down? What the bleeding—'

'I said pipe down. I'll hold everything ten minutes. The lads aren't off yet. You beat the gun by exactly fifteen seconds. Now. Get a substitute – understand me – and follow the original route. Ten-fifteen instead of ten-five. Got that?'

'O.K. But I haven't a clue where—'

Rapid suggestions poured out of the receiver. He took in as many as he could, slammed back the instrument and hurried off.

Not far from the Town Hall in Chelsea he found a cul-de-sac with a long block of flats. In this private road the cars of the tenants were parked side by side facing outwards. A very convenient take-off.

7

The man who had abandoned the crippled Jaguar found a black Humber in the row. He juggled swiftly with the bunch of ignition keys that he took from his pocket. The car door opened, he got in quickly and drove out of the cul-de-sac, back into the King's Road, round the next corner into Oakley Street and across the river by the Albert Bridge.

He began to breathe more slowly and more freely. The hurried walk along the King's Road had disturbed him in more ways than one. He was not used to walking, particularly at a rapid pace. His physical exercise was taken for the most part sitting; in vans, in lorries, in cars as now. With occasional spells, up to a couple of years, moving round an exercise yard, standing at benches, or even sitting in a row with a needle between his fingers and a mailbag on his lap. But never walking fast or running, if he could help it. Though he was not of a heavy build, being on the contrary a thin, loosely made individual, with narrow rounded shoulders, he could stand neither the effort nor the frighteningly slow pace of movement on his own two legs. After a car it felt like paralysis, he used to complain aloud at times. He complained now, under his breath, as the Humber shot across Albert Bridge and on in the direction of Lavender Hill. The rendezvous was in a back street near the big store at the crossroads.

It was not to be a rendezvous in the ordinary sense of the word. The 'blocking' van would be in the street at the kerb, with one man, the driver, only. The other van with the three in it would drive past. So would he. They would circle the block in opposite directions. When they got back the car they were waiting for should be moving just ahead and the 'blocking' van should be taking off across its course.

He turned into the street. It was fairly long. It had been chosen partly to give a clear view but chiefly because the wages car always used it to approach the back entrance of the store. This car came down another side street from the bank. It always reached the bank just after ten and got back to the store not later than ten-fifteen. They were cutting it pretty fine with the ten-minute delay.

He looked at his watch and swore. He was late. Even on the new schedule he was late. It made him nervy, so that he hesitated before completing his turn, looking quickly up and down the street.

He was late, all right. The whole thing had come unstuck. With a ghastly picture in his mind of what he had just seen, he drove straight across the street into the one opposite, zigzagged back to the main road beyond the lights at the corner and went on, swearing, sweating, wondering where and how it would be safe to get rid of the Humber. There was going to be another walk. Another bloody walk. And later, the reckoning.

He considered again what he had seen.

The lads had carried on as if he was expected. That was obvious. They couldn't have got any messages about holding off ten minutes. Perhaps the store's car had been a bit early. That could be it. They'd worked to schedule and boxed the car all right. He'd seen the three vehicles close together. A small crowd standing on the pavement. A group of the law, surrounding two figures he couldn't distinguish. A police car and worst of all, a police van.

He hadn't waited to sort out this scene. He'd been too scared. But he tried to sort it out now as he drove on towards Putney. It made sense all right. He was the missing piece in the game. They'd expected him and he wasn't there. Well, why had they gone on? Wasn't there always the check? Why had they gone on without checking he was there?

He found an answer to that, too. They hadn't got a message so they didn't know he'd switched cars. Some other Jag must have passed them on the check and they'd taken it for him. Of all the rotten luck!

He turned off into Garratt's Lane. He knew this part of London in the dark, in his sleep. He smiled faintly as he passed the juvenile court room, scene of four, or was it five, of his early appearances.

He turned down another side street, drew up a little beyond a small tobacconist and newsagent and left the Humber, unlocked, at the kerb. There would be no ignition key in it, but if some enterprising tearaway could rustle one up to give himself a ride, so much the better.

He left the car, he walked into the tobacconist, bought a morning paper and another packet of cigarettes, lit one as he left the shop, took a bus into Putney and from there got on the Underground. He was at Paddington by eleven. In the early afternoon he was in Reading, where he had a widowed mother, who had been evacuated there in the later years of the war and had stayed on afterwards. She could always be frightened into supporting his alibis. Not that it often did him much good. He thought that on this occasion it might.

Later in the day he bought an evening paper. The failed raid had a paragraph on the front page. This made him mad. The cops were patting themselves on the back. With the help of two interfering members of the public – and he'd see they got done when he'd identified them as witnesses in court – two men had been detained, two had got away. He wondered which were the unlucky ones.

There was nothing in the paper about the Humber. Nor about the Jag. But he didn't expect it. Normally it took anything up to two days before the law came on abandoned cars, unless they had a clear description from the owner. Not always then. But there wouldn't be any description this time, at least not of the Jag; its owner was abroad.

He decided to stop over a week. After that he'd go back and tell Burt – *Mister* Burt he liked to be called – that he hadn't found a second car for the job, so he'd packed it in. It wasn't his fault. The Jag had been just the ticket. Owner going abroad, no complaint about it, wouldn't be missed for days. It was sheer bad luck the tyre had burst. It hadn't occurred to him the boys would try to carry on without support. That wasn't his fault, either, was it?

CHAPTER TWO

THE Jaguar stood in front of the house all day. From time to time the woman who had seen it arrive went to her window to look out. She was puzzled, but it did not occur to her to do anything about it. When she went out to shop she met her neighbour from the next floor up coming in. They had a few words about the car.

'Yeh. I see it when I went out. That'd be just an hour ago. I thought, what next? Surely she hasn't flown as high as that?'

The woman on the ground floor understood this veiled remark. It referred to the top floor back, where a young woman, calling herself a model, came home late to sleep in the house, but was seldom seen otherwise.

'Nothing to do with 'er. Not this time. And a good thing, too. I'd not stand for it if she brought them back to the 'ouse. Bad enough her coming in with the milk and stopping up there all day. No, this chap parked at the door and walked off. Cool as a cucumber and not even a passing glance at the damage. Naturally I thought 'e'd gone to find a garridge. But no one's been.'

'That's funny. Supposing it don't belong to 'im.'

'The car?'

'Yeh. One of these joy-riders.'

'Couldn't say. It's not my business.'

They shrugged and parted, Mrs. Wilton making her way to the shops in the King's Road, while her neighbour went upstairs. Neither of them gave another thought to the Jaguar.

In the afternoon the children came home from school. Some of the older boys stopped when they saw the crippled car. They inspected the flat tyre, they peered through the windows at the fine leather seats, the folded fur rug, the row of control knobs on the dashboard, the dials above.

At first they kept a lookout for the owner, but presently one boy said, 'Must 'ave been 'ere *hours*. Road's dry under.'

They all stooped and looked. It was true. The shower that had come down at the end of the morning and stopped them going into the playground after dinner had wetted the roads and pavements and the shining paint of the Jag, but underneath the car there was no sign of rain at all.

'Coo! Been 'ere all day!'

'Crackers! With a flat tyre an all.'

'May've went down after.'

'Wot d'you mean? After it were left?'

'Why not?'

Confidence grew when it appeared to be definite that the car had been abandoned. Older boys continued to stop to inspect and admire. Younger boys and girls began to play games round it. One or two got pencils or chalks from their satchels and wrote or drew lines on the bonnet and the boot.

Presently a policeman on a motor scooter came down the street, patrolling his beat. He drew in to the kerb. The younger children ran off screaming in mock terror or laughing at those who screamed. One or two of the older boys held their ground.

'Did you do this damage?' the constable asked. He was young and his face grew pink as he spoke. His audience gazed at him, summing him up, treating him to a frank scorn that made him grow pinker still.

'Lost your tongues?' he barked at them.

'It's bin 'ere since the morning, mister,' said the boy who had worked this out. 'And the front tyre's down.'

'Who did that?'

'Better ask the owner.'

'Where is he?'

The boys had begun to move away. The constable, realizing that his question was a foolish one, ignored them, bending instead to look under the car. He remembered the rain himself and the time it had fallen. This Jag with its flat tyre had been here since before eleven that morning. He walked up the steps of the house in front of which the car was parked and rang the bottom bell.

Mrs. Wilton came from her back room where she had been watching the tele. She was not at all pleased to be disturbed, especially as she was not expecting a visitor and had on previous occasions answered the bell at this time of day only to find it had been rung by schoolchildren on their way home. Most probably the young devils at it again now, she thought, as she opened the door.

The uniform on the doorstep gave her quite a shock. Her inclination was to say at once, defensively, 'She isn't in'. Then she remembered that the model might not yet be known to the law, so she said nothing, just held the door, partly closed, waiting.

'Can you tell me, madam,' said the young constable, growing very pink indeed, 'if the owner of this car is in the house?'

Mrs. Wilton looked him up and down with more open scorn even than the schoolboys.

'Would you expect the owner of that car to be in this house?' she asked.

The constable was nettled. He knew he had not handled the schoolboys very well. This was a lot worse.

'I'm never surprised at anything,' he said, sharply. 'I take it the car is not yours?'

'You trying to be funny?'

'Now look, madam,' the constable tried again. 'This car has been left in front of your house with a flat front tyre since some time this morning and—'

'If you know all that why haven't you done something about it before now?'

'Sometime this morning,' repeated the constable, hanging on to his temper with both hands. 'And—'

'Nine-thirty or thereabouts,' said Mrs. Wilton.

'You saw it arrive?'

She nodded.

'Dusting my front room. Drove up sudden. Young fellow got out and walked off.'

'Why didn't you say so before?'

'You didn't ask me.'

The constable swallowed. He tried to remember what he had been taught about not antagonizing witnesses.

'No, I didn't, did I?'

'You not bin in the Force long, 'ave you?' said Mrs Wilton, not in the least mollified.

The constable swallowed again, but he persisted.

'What did he look like? The owner of the car, I mean?'

' 'Ow do I know 'e was the owner? Doesn't look much like it to me. Goes off and leaves a valuable machine like that – not even taking a look at the damage—'

'Go on.'

'Well, use your loaf. Would *you* say 'e was the owner?'

'Whoever he was, what did he look like? Or didn't you notice?'

The constable instantly regretted this qualifying phrase, but in fact it was the best thing he could have said. Mrs. Wilton's first reaction had been to have nothing to do with the business, to keep out at all costs. But her pride was touched.

'Course I noticed. Thin, long 'air, sloppy-like. Not the sort I'd expect in that type of car.'

'Dark or fair?'

'Middling.'

'Tall or short?'

'Neither. Just thin, stooped a bit. Not 'arf in a 'urry.

Though I must say 'e did stop to lock it up. And fetch a packet of fags out of 'is pocket, too.'

The constable, who had not made the elementary examination necessary to establish the first of these facts, blushed again.

'May I have your name and—' He looked at the number of the house; he knew the street.

'Your name, Mrs—'

'Wilton,' she said, reluctantly, with a vision of the magistrate's court ahead.

'Thank you, madam,' the constable said, formally, turning away. Mrs. Wilton shut the door on him almost before the words were out.

About an hour later the official breakdown van arrived. The Jaguar was hoisted up and borne away. The young constable, who was present during this operation, took a look at the dry patch of roadway where the car had stopped. He found there a crumpled cigarette carton which he picked up and presented to a sergeant at his police station when he went off duty.

'What's this in aid of?' the sergeant asked, looking at the torn relic with disfavour.

'I thought it might be his. The driver's, I mean. Mrs. Wilton said he got a packet of cigarettes out of his pocket before he walked off. I thought—'

'O.K. I can do simple arithmetic, too.'

The Jaguar was unloaded at the pound. Its registration number and particulars had already been turned in by the constable and recorded and the police found, with some surprise, that there had been no inquiry as to its whereabouts. As the constable's story seemed to indicate that the car had been stolen, this was surprising. Further inquiries were put in train.

Chelsea as well as Fulham was troubled with car thefts that day, though with cars removed, not with cars dumped in the area. Of four missing vehicles notified by the owners during the morning, a black Humber was located in the early afternoon in a street off Garratt Lane in Wandsworth. The owner was able to state, within fifteen minutes, the time it was stolen. He had gone out to his garage to fetch it, driven it to the cul-de-sac in front of the flats where he lived and parked it there while he went indoors to get some additional papers he had forgotten to put in his brief-case. He had done this between nine and nine-fifteen. Just after nine-thirty he had gone out again to find the Humber was missing.

These details, too, went up to the Information Room at Scotland Yard and were duly recorded. A look at the big map devoted to car thefts, together with the pinned-in details of raids and other crimes raised some interesting speculations. They seemed to explain why the raid near Lavender Hill had collapsed so strangely.

And still, twelve hours after the Jaguar had been parked with a flat tyre, no one had notified its absence, no one had made any inquiries about it at all.

The later editions of the evening papers splashed the failed raid even more lavishly than the earlier ones.

It had been a triumph, the column roared, of quick wits and initiative and courage on the part of a public too long apathetic in face of the mounting crime wave. The thieves had shut in the wages van between another van, driven suddenly from the kerb and the car in which were three masked men. These three, with the driver of the first van, had jumped out to attack the two men with the wages. But a car coming up behind had deliberately blocked the raiding car. Moreover the driver of this car had jumped out and gone for the four men single-handed, hitting out right and left with an umbrella he had with him. He broke it over one head and drove the broken end into the stomach of another man, winding him. Inspired by this magnifi-cent action, a pedestrian had joined him in the fray. The thieves seemed to be taken completely off guard. They were darting wildly, in a demoralized fashion, up and down the road. They had abandoned their spoils and seemed to be intent only on escape. They

had clearly lost their heads, because at first escape
down side streets would have been comparatively easy.
A police patrol car arrived very quickly on the scene,
summoned by a member of the staff of the big store,
whose windows overlooked the street. Two arrests
were made.

The column ended with a reference to the Binney
Medal, awarded for gallantry in assisting the police
in their duty.

In a public house in Notting Hill the survivors of the
gang sat drinking despondently and reading this
account of their morning's disappointment.

'The public be—' O'Hara expressed his contempt in
a few rude phrases. 'It was nothing to do with them.
It was Len. Everything was as right as rain till he
didn't show up with the car. And for why didn't he
do that? When the check went through as smooth as
silk?'

'He 'as not come,' said Corri, with a glint in the
dark eyes he turned sideways on his companion. 'If
it was the car at fault in those two-three minutes, 'e
would be 'ere now for the explanation. 'E let us down.'

O'Hara shook his head in bewilderment. 'It's not
like Len. I worked with 'im before. I never known 'im
go back on a thing once 'e started it. Not deliberate,
like this.'

'Now we 'ave Mr. Burt,' said Corri. 'Now we know
what 'appen.'

A short, stoutish man had just come into the pub.
He went up to the bar, bought packet of cigarettes
and a small whisky, drank the latter in two gulps and
walked out again. The men at the table finished their
drinks and followed him. There was a car in the road
with Mr. Burt at the wheel and the engine running.
O'Hara and Corri got in without a word and they
drove off.

In Mr. Burt's comfortable sitting-room the failure
of the raid was made plain.

'I shall *not* work with your lot again,' Mr. Burt said,

with cold precise emphasis. 'You did *not* take the elementary precaution of synchronizing your watches. Elementary – and essential. You must have left your base quite five minutes before the agreed deadline.'

The two remained silent.

'As for Len,' said Mr. Burt. 'I've not made up my mind about him. His story of a burst tyre may be complete poppycock.'

'So that was the trouble!' burst out O'Hara. 'And when did that happen, may I ask?'

'Within a few minutes of the deadline. I rang you at once, but you'd left. There was nothing more I could do.'

'Couldn't 'e 'ave rustled up another car?'

'That was what I suggested to him. Apparently he did not, since no car arrived for you.'

' 'Ow do you know it did not arrive?' Corri asked, sullenly. 'You was not there. You keep out of sight. You – sit pretty – no?'

'Have you not had a word from Len since?' asked O'Hara, anxiously.

'Not a word. Moreover he's left town.'

'Gone to 'is old ma in Reading, I wouldn't wonder,' suggested the Irishman. Then seeing Mr. Burt's sudden interest he opened his small blue eyes wide and remarked innocently, in a prim imitation of the other, 'Were you not aware of his home life, Mr. Burt?'

'What's the address?' Burt already had a pencil and old envelope ready.

'Oh, I wouldn't be knowing that,' said O'Hara with a smile. ' 'E's not the confiding sort, Len. Is he, Mr. Burt? I just happened to hear 'im pass the remark that 'is ma was in Reading and 'e was in the habit of visiting the old woman from time to time to cheer her up.'

Mr. Burt was baffled and he did not like it. He changed the subject.

'Two bags were taken from the van,' he said. 'One was bust open. Any pickings?'

O'Hara shook his head and sighed.

'Not a cent,' he said, sadly.

Mr. Burt looked at Corri. The man's blue jowl was thrust forward. His dark eyes stared coldly at the boss.

'Then you can both get out!' said Mr. Burt, in a sudden rise of temper. 'Get out, the useless pair of you!'

Corri got up and stood over Mr. Burt, his eyes no longer cold, but glinting with rage.

'You talk big, mister,' he said. 'Maybe the mistake not Len, but *you*. Our watches was correct – *correct*, I say. Maybe your watch *slow*. You call us *after* the time we start. *You* let *us* down, Mr. Burt. You not so big boss maybe.'

If Mr. Burt was afraid he did not show it. He stood quite still, but the hand he always kept in his jacket pocket moved a little. O'Hara, seeing this, plucked at Corri's sleeve.

'He's upset, Mr. Burt,' he said, apologetically. 'Come away there, my boyo.'

Mr. Burt saw them out of the flat himself and locked and chained the door when they had gone. He was white with rage and frustration, but not fear. He was pretty certain now that O'Hara had saved a little something for himself from the raid, perhaps Corri, too, though the latter was a slow thinker, useful only when brawn was needed. Since O'Hara had profited he would not be likely to grass. Nor, certainly, would Ed and Ray. They were new recruits as far as he was concerned and had never actually seen him. Nor did they know where he really lived, though Len had brought them once to the flat.

For that matter, neither did O'Hara, Corri or Len know where he really lived. At this thought Mr. Burt smiled, put on his overcoat and left. He turned his car and drove it away to the car-hire garage from which he had got it. Then he made his way by public transport to the house in a south London suburb where, under quite a different name, his wife lived and was now waiting for him to return from the office.

CHAPTER THREE

THE Jaguar, it was discovered, belonged to a certain Sir John Drewson, of Drews Court Cottage, Southfield, Sussex. Inquiries at his home brought the news that he was abroad. He had left Drews Court early in the morning on the previous day, to drive direct to London Airport. His housekeeper had no further details to add. Asked if Sir John was travelling alone she answered in a shocked voice that of course his secretary, Mrs. Wood, had gone with him. Mrs. Wood had arrived at the cottage the evening before. The housekeeper had got breakfast at six in the morning for the two of them. They had left at seven. She understood the plane was due to take off at nine or thereabouts.

This was enlightening. The Jaguar had clearly been taken from London Airport. But had Sir John simply parked it there, expecting to find it on his return? There were a good many more questions that needed answers. Where had he gone? When was he due back? Mrs. Heath was vague in her answers.

'We don't even know what flight he was on, yet,' said the traffic police inspector detailed to clear up the case. Sir John Drewson, it seemed, was a person of some importance. The matter of his car had been given a certain priority. Apart from the fact that it might be tied in with the wages raid that hadn't come off.

'I'm going down to the airport. See if I can sort some of this out.'

It took him half the morning to do so, but he got the facts he wanted. Sir John had flown by B.E.A. to Zürich. He was staying in Switzerland three days and had booked his return flight for Tuesday next, this being Saturday of the third week in October. So much for dates. The customs and immigration officers were mildly enlightening. Sir John travelled abroad fairly often to attend conferences, they understood. Usually he had his secretary with him.

'What's she like?'

'Tall. Fortyish. Ugly as sin.'

The inspector did not express disappointment, though he felt a passing twinge, more on Sir John's account than any other.

'Know anything about these conferences? Political?'

'No. Welfare of some sort. Look, don't you read the papers? Haven't you ever heard of this bloke? He's some sort of public benefactor.'

'We're a bit too occupied with the opposite sort,' said the inspector, testily.

But he decided that he could do with a bit more information about Drewson. If the chap was not due back for three days, something would have to be done about his car. It didn't sound quite like a public character with that kind of secretary to be quite so casual over a valuable car. And there was another thing. The address he had used at the airport was not the same as the one under which the car was registered. It was quite normal for a man in Sir John's position to have two addresses, but he proposed to check.

The second address, confirmed by the London telephone directory, took the inspector to a block of flats near Ebury Street. Sir John certainly rented one of the smaller flats in this block. He usually spent one or two nights a week in town. The caretaker spoke of him with great respect, but with evident curiosity.

'Sir John informed me when he returned to the country on Thursday, two days ago, that he would not be here again until the end of next week. He had a conference to attend in Switzerland.'

'So I understand. Tell me, where does Sir John keep his car when he's in town?'

'He never hardly brings it to London. Scared of the traffic these days. He must be nearly sixty, come to think of it. No, I've never seen him bring the car into

London himself, and he has no garage here for it, that I know of.'

'But you have seen the car?'

'Oh yes, when Miss Tollet drives him up, occasionally. Then she leaves it in the street outside if she can find a place.'

'Who is Miss Tollet?'

'Sir John's niece. He's very fond of her. She might be his daughter the way he spoils her.'

'Can you give me her address?'

'I can tell you where she works.'

'She works, does she?'

The caretaker was becoming more cautious. He was willing to oblige the law. He had found it advisable in the past, in connection with more than one of the more transitory tenants, not to be too cagey with the police. Besides, it made for variety and interest. He had always been one to take an interest in other people.

So now he said, a little anxiously, 'There's nothing wrong, is there? I wouldn't like the young lady to get into trouble?'

'Do you think she's the kind that might? What sort of trouble?'

'There's no need to pick me up so quick. I never said anything in connection with Miss Tollet. High-spirited and a bit spoiled, like I said. But a very nice young lady, really. I wouldn't like to think, after giving you her business address—'

'There's nothing for you to worry about.'

With that the caretaker had to be content, but once or twice in the next hour he wondered if he had been right to give Miss Tollet's address. Such a nice young lady. He didn't want her to get into trouble. But there had been those times she'd borrowed the Jag without her uncle knowing. The old boy had found out once and flared up over it. Quite unlike him, that. But he must have made it up with her because she kept on coming to see him and he left messages for her to meet him for dinner or the theatre. So it ought to be all right.

Two hours later the inspector, after a hasty lunch, was back at Scotland Yard to report. He was not quite sure that Miss Tollet had spoken the truth to him.

He had found her at the publishing firm in Bloomsbury where she worked as secretary to one of the directors. It was just after noon when he called there and the office was obviously on the point of closing down for the weekend. He was put into a very small waiting-room, two of whose walls were furnished with tall bookshelves filled with early products of the firm. The third wall was covered with signed photographs, mostly faded, of distinguished authors of the past who had supplied the manuscripts for the books on the shelves.

The inspector was not interested in books or he might have wondered why there were no photographs of the modern best-selling authors whose works were displayed on a table near the fourth wall, under the closed windows. He might have decided that though their present value to the firm was immense, their future value in prestige was not yet established.

After nearly twenty minutes Belinda Tollet joined the inspector in the waiting-room. She was twenty-five and looked younger. She had a reasonably fashionable mass of naturally wavy hair of a natural dark auburn colour. Her skin was creamy, her dark eyebrows delicate, her lashes also dark and naturally long, her eyes a very deep blue. Her make-up was pleasing and did not suggest that she was suffering either from early jaundice or the last stages of leukaemia. She was beautifully dressed and ready to leave. The inspector felt a glow of deepest approval, instantly controlled.

'I'm sorry to inconvenience you, miss,' he began. 'It's about Sir John Drewson's car. You are his niece, I understand, and he is abroad?'

'Yes, I am,' Belinda said, opening the blue eyes very wide. 'And he is. *What* about Uncle John's car?'

'We have it in the pound,' the inspector said, simply,

and added, 'there's a puncture in the nearside front tyre.'

'Come again.'

The inspector repeated his statement, adding this time, 'I understand that Sir John is not expected back until next Tuesday.'

'Oh, *hell!*'

Miss Tollet's heartfelt exclamation surprised the inspector but his training kept him from showing it. He merely waited.

'Look,' said the girl carefully. 'Can I simply claim it myself, get the wheel changed and drive it away? I'll pay the fine, if there is any.'

'Without Sir John's authorization that would not be in order, miss.'

'But I don't want him to *know*. The whole point is he should *not* know what's happened.'

'Perhaps you could tell *me* what's happened. Then I might be able to advise you.'

'Oh, don't be so pompous! The thing is this. Uncle John had to get to the airport very early in the morning. He was taking Mrs. Wood, that's his secretary, with him, so she couldn't cope with the car. He was going up from Drews Court, that's where he lives in Sussex. In the cottage that used to be the lodge. *So*, he asked me to go down and drive the car away from the airport and park it somewhere in London till I finished work and then run it down to Southfield.'

'But you got a puncture. Why did you leave—?'

'Oh, let me finish! *I* didn't get the puncture. I didn't even go to the airport. I overslept.'

'Indeed.'

The inspector's face expressed strong disbelief. Miss Tollet was exasperated.

'What's so unlikely about that? I'd had a *very* late night the day before. And I didn't oversleep by much. I got here just after ten. My usual time is nine-thirty, but my boss never arrives till ten or after.'

'So you didn't drive the car away from London Airport?'

'I've just told you.'

'Then who did?'

Miss Tollet's face reddened, then grew very pale. The blue eyes were clouded now.

'When I saw I wasn't going to be able to make it I rang up a friend of mine and asked him to collect instead and let me know later where the Jag was.'

'And then?'

'He didn't. I mean, I was working and I don't like him to call me here, but there was no message when I got home.'

'Where is home?'

Miss Tollet gave her address in West Hampstead where she shared a flat with two girl-friends.

'What did you conclude when you received no message?'

'That he'd got the Jag and taken it down to South-field on his own.'

'Wouldn't that be a very strange thing to do? Without letting you know?'

'Not terribly. There's a friend of his who has left London to live in the south somewhere. Hugh may have wanted to see him.'

'Even so—'

'I don't like this friend. He makes my skin crawl, if you know what I mean. I shouldn't wonder if he's a crook of some sort. Hugh says I've no right to think beastly things about him.'

'Your friend's name?' asked the inspector, refusing to be led off on side lines.

'Hugh's? Mellanby. He's a barrister. At least, I don't think he gets any briefs of his own yet, but he's been called to the bar and he works, if you can call it that, in chambers belonging to Mr. Warrington-Reeve.'

'I've heard of *him*,' the inspector said. It was only a

few months since the well-known counsel had secured the acquittal of a suspected murderer.

'I thought you might,' Miss Tollet answered, sweetly.

'So you think Mr. Mellanby collected the Jaguar and was intending to drive it down to Southfield without informing you of his intention?'

'No, I don't,' said Miss Tollet, firmly. 'Not now there was a puncture. Hugh would have changed the wheel, himself. He'd never have just walked off, without a word to anyone, then or since.'

The inspector got up. He did not feel quite sure about Miss Tollet. She had been rather too fluent. Rather too full of suggestions that amounted to nothing.

'You think someone stole it, don't you?' she said, as she opened the door for him. 'I wish you'd let me just collect it. I was asked to, wasn't I?'

'We should need Sir John's authorization for that,' the inspector repeated.

He hurried away. He might just manage to catch young Mr. Mellanby before he left his Inn. That is if the young man was keen enough to work on Saturday. Mr. Warrington-Reeve usually kept his youngsters hard at it, so he'd been told.

Miss Tollet, after seeing the inspector off the premises, found the office deserted except for the porter, who was tying up a few book parcels while he waited to lock up the place. She had been ready to go when she was called to the waiting-room, so she had no excuse for going up again to her own office. She said goodbye to the porter and ran down the steps, hurried to the call-box on the corner, rang up Hugh at his chambers and was both comforted and enraged to hear his voice answering quite calmly from the other end. She poured out her story in a stream of short, graphic sentences.

'But I *did* go,' Hugh protested. 'I went and I searched the damned park from end to end three times. I then concluded that you'd gone down after all, so I came away.'

'It didn't occur to you to ring me up and say so?'

'You don't like being called at your office. Besides, I did try to ring you at home and got no answer.'

'Yes. Sorry. We were all out.'

'I expected *you* to ring *me*.'

'So the poor old Jag was pinched and left with a flat tyre somewhere.'

'Don't you know where?'

'D'you think the inspector would tell me a simple fact like that? He was all blown up with suspicion. Like a toad.'

'Come, come. You can do better than that.'

'Oh, go to hell!'

She was about to slam back the receiver but Hugh's voice, pleading, stopped her hand.

'*Darling!* So *touchy*! Have you had lunch?'

'No. Of course not. My third degree has only just—'

'O.K. Meet me in ten minutes. Usual place. No! Hold it!'

She could hear a voice in the background. Then Hugh again, more urgent still.

'Linda! Listen! Your inspector's on the threshold. Make it half an hour.'

'I shall starve. But I'll be there. 'Bye.'

The inspector was quite sure, from the agitated movements of young Mr. Mellanby and the guilty look he cast first at the telephone and then at his visitor that he himself was three minutes too late and his opportunity for getting an independent account had melted.

But he persisted, nevertheless, encouraging the barrister to give him a clear and detailed account of his search for the Jaguar and the exact wording of Miss Tollet's request to go to the airport. He did learn one fact that the girl had not given him, which was that Sir John would probably have parked the car not later than eight in the morning. He always allowed one hour at the airport before the time of his flight. So Miss Tollet would have had time, if she had got up early enough, to go down and bring the Jaguar into town before she was due at the office. On his way to see Mellanby this problem had worried the inspector. It did nothing to ease his task now. Mellanby had not gone to look for the Jag until the end of the morning. But knowing when it had been left in Fulham it could have been stolen between eight and nine. Therefore it need not have been driven straight there from the airport.

'Where is the Jag now?' Hugh asked at the end of the inspector's questioning. Off guard, preoccupied with his time speculations, the officer told him.

'Stolen, of course?'

'You might call it that. What makes you think so, sir?'

'Cars of that type are used to make getaways in raids, aren't they? My paper tells me there was a raid yesterday that didn't come off because there was no getaway car. Puncture in the Jag. Link – no?'

'Why should you pick on this particular damaged car, sir? Damage is a daily occurrence in the case of joy-riding borrowed cars.'

'Joy-riders don't go out to the airport to look for vehicles. They get into anything handy in the street. And you told me where the Jag is now. That narrows the district where you found it, which you have been careful not to tell me. But it must be in the area of that raid or not far off.'

'You are making progress in your profession, sir, if I may say so,' said the inspector, with a return of his pompous manner that took away any slight sting there was in his intended sarcasm.

'Thank you. Now, if you have no more questions, officer, I have a lunch date.'

'Should you see Miss Tollet, sir,' the inspector told him, 'you might inform her that we shall be in communication with Sir John in regard to the Jaguar. She may like to know that, in the circumstances.'

When Hugh repeated this to Belinda at lunch a little later she was considerably upset.

'That's torn it completely,' she said, furiously. 'I'll have to get in first and it'll cost the earth ringing up his hotel.'

"You needn't say you passed the buck to me,' Hugh suggested. 'Simply say the car was taken from the airport park, you don't know who by. So you couldn't drive it down to Drews Court for him. How were you supposed to get back from there? You had to work on Friday, hadn't you? You wouldn't have been able to start down till the evening.'

'I know. I thought it was a bit much when he asked me. But he's such a dear, really. He's done so much for me. I think he's so used to being kind to other people and helping them in every possible way that he thinks it's quite natural for people to be ready to do things occasionally for him.'

Hugh seemed to have something on his mind, not to have taken in quite Belinda's eulogy of her uncle.

'What is it?' she asked.

'What is what?'

'You aren't listening. You're worried. What about?'

He tried to laugh, but failed. He stared at her with solemn, troubled eyes.

'I think, on the whole, you had better tell him the whole story. The police will, anyhow, don't you see?'

'Yes.'

Belinda agreed, but she was not convinced that this was the whole cause of Hugh's abstraction. She did not press him for an explanation, however, but continued to eat her lunch in silence. When they had finished their meal and travelled by bus to Hugh's lodgings in a dingy building off the Gray's Inn Road, her forbearance was rewarded.

'What about your call to Zürich?' he asked.

'I wondered if Mrs. Cole would let me do it from here? We can ask for the charge and I'll give it her straight away. We shall have to wait to get through.'

'We can ask her.'

Mrs. Cole was agreeable. The call was put in hand and presently Belinda was through, asking to speak to Sir John. But he was out. Belinda gave a message in very inadequate French and said she would write a letter explaining detail.

'All that good "mon" down the drain,' she complained. 'I suppose I'd better go home and write the letter.'

'Come for a drive first. Anywhere you like. It's much too good an afternoon to waste indoors.'

So they went round to the mews where Hugh kept his battered but mechanically sound car, and as they drove out of London, heading south, he explained at last the load on his mind.

'I've been meaning to tell you,' he began, keeping his eyes very strictly on the road ahead. 'I saw Sir John the night before he left.'

'You saw him? Where?'

'At Southfield. At the cottage.'

'On Thursday! When?'

'Listen, darling. And don't interrupt. And don't get angry. I went down to Southfield on Thursday evening to see Jeremy.'

Belinda made an audible sound of disgust.

'No. I said don't get angry or I won't go on.'

'Sorry. Please go on.'

'I know you can't stand Jeremy at any price, but—'

'He makes my skin crawl.'

'O.K. If you don't want to listen—'

They drove on in silence for a few minutes then Belinda said, 'Hugh darling, please go on. I won't interrupt again.'

'I was at Oxbridge with him as I've told you umpteen times. He was very bright, very unsure of himself, very open to every kind of influence. I liked him my first year. He seemed to be settling down and finding his feet. I saw less of him my second year. He was still reading law but I had my own friends by then and I didn't like his. He seemed to have got in with a very doubtful crowd. In the middle of my third year he was sent down and he never took a degree.'

'What had he done?'

'I don't know. I never asked him.'

'But there must have been rumours. That sort of thing always gets out. Didn't anyone put up a fight for him? What about those friends?'

'No one tried to do anything for him. There were rumours all right. All the usual ones and a few even more exotic. I didn't think myself it was anything to do with sex. More likely money.'

'Why did you go on knowing him?'

'He wrote to me. He was pretty desperate.'

'And then?'

Hugh did not answer at once. Then he said, 'Oh, various things. He went into journalism. Free-lance crime reporting. He was quite qualified to do this. Lately he's given it up. Took to writing a novel, apparently. Anyway, buried himself in the country in a pretty dim bungalow he says he owns, at South-field, about a mile and a half from Drews Court.'

'Oh, *no*!'

Belinda, who had only met Jeremy Ditchling at parties in London, was shocked to find the unspeakable one lived near her uncle, but was very curious to hear the rest of Hugh's story.

'Was that why you saw Uncle John on Friday? I don't get the connection.'

'It was. The connection is that Jeremy wasn't at home, though he'd asked me to go down.'

'And so?'

'He'd asked me to dinner. His bungalow door was – unlocked. I walked in and called but there was no answer. No Jeremy. No sign of food. Nothing.'

'But why go to Uncle John?'

'Jeremy knew him. He has a way of getting to know people.'

'Don't I know? Tagging on to junior literary circles.

After what you've said I'm quite surprised he was at some of those parties where I had to meet him.'

'Quite. But it wasn't altogether push on his part, his knowing Sir John. I'd asked his advice about Jeremy once and later they met. I thought it just possible he might be at the cottage.'

'And was he?'

'No. But he had been. Sir John said he had been, but had left half an hour before, by the footpath over the fields. That would account for my missing him. I went by the road.'

'Well?'

'Well, your uncle asked me in for a drink but I said I'd better be getting back to the bungalow. However, he insisted, so I had a quick one and then Mrs. Wood arrived, so I left.'

'But Jeremy still wasn't there when you got back?'

'No.'

'I suppose he knew Uncle John was going abroad?'

'Obviously. He'd be sure to find that out.'

'So you think he may have gone to town that night and stolen the Jag in the morning?'

'I wouldn't put it past him. He's always been a bit crazy and he's got steadily more and more scatty and more and more nervy. I would have thought, though, that he'd give me dinner as arranged and get me to drive him into town. He's always been a first-class scrounger.'

'I bet. What are you really worried about, Hugh?'

'I'd like to know what he's up to.'

'Does it matter to you – personally, I mean?'

Hugh turned his eyes to her then and she saw the wild anxiety in them and felt a sharp thrill of fear run through her.

'Perhaps he's back at home,' she said. 'If he took the Jag it can't have been much use to him.'

'I wonder.'

Belinda looked out at the passing countryside. 'We're going to Southfield now, aren't we?' she said.

'If you don't mind?'

'If he's there I can say I came down to see Mrs. Heath at the cottage and simply walk away,' she answered.

CHAPTER FOUR

OF the two young men captured in the abortive raid the older was more helpful to the police than his companion.

The younger one, Ed Bale, pointed out that there was nothing to connect him with the raid at all. He was parked at the kerb, he drew out into what he thought was a clear road and this car ran into him. He got out to take particulars of the accident and then these three men piled out of a car at the rear of the car that had rammed him and the next he knew he was being beaten up by the bloody rozzers—

'You can drop that line. You weren't hurt and you've nothing to show. You came quietly.'

He had and he knew he had. It was standard form to say the law had been brutal.

'I was taking my van out from the kerb.'

'Where did you get it?'

'That's rich, that is. The van? It's my boss's van. I just got back with the load. I'm telling you. It was all legitimate.'

'Why were you parked?'

'Ever 'eard of public toilets, mister?'

Unfortunately, from the police point of view, Ed was found to be speaking the truth, at least in part. The van did indeed belong to the small greengrocer at whose shop he worked. He was indeed on his way back to the shop from the market, though he was a good half hour late.

'He always says the traffic was bad,' his worried employer explained. 'It could be, couldn't it? He's a good lad, is Ed. Never pinches the fruit and that, even at strawberry time.'

'He has bigger ideas, perhaps.'

'He could be speaking the truth about the toilets, couldn't he?'

'Unfortunately, yes.'

They were going to have to let Ed go, this time. Perhaps there was just a chance it might be a lesson to him. It was the first time he had come their way, though they were pretty sure it was not his first offence. He'd had a considerable shock. He might not feel so big; for a bit, anyway.

The other lad, Ray, was different. He was an overgrown, brutish looking lout of twenty. He tried speaking in the soft, menacing voice of his kind until the divisional detective-inspector told him sharply to speak up and try to speak clearly, if he could. His normal response to this insult was instant attack, but it did him no good at all. He found himself held in a grip that prevented the use of all his choicer methods and that he was quite powerless to break. He found himself a few minutes later handcuffed and sitting by himself in a small cell. He tried kicking the next time he was visited. This only meant that the tea and biscuits he was being brought were taken away in fragments and a long wait ensued. The next time he was called he went sullenly, expecting the worst.

However, the handcuffs were removed and he was again offered tea and biscuits. He said nothing but reached for them. He was hungry and the shock of his arrest had made him very thirsty, too.

He did, however, make a last effort to assert his superiority, his total rejection of the law. When the inspector leaned forward a little later to begin his questions, Ray spat full in his face.

This time he found himself alone until the next morning, except for one visit when a cup of cocoa and two thick slices of bread and butter were handed in to him. He lay on the hard bed in his cell, tortured by the

silence, by the lack of company, by the present un-
certainty of his fate, by the memory of people in the
street laughing – laughing, the b—s, when he was
pushed struggling – was he really upside down? – into
the black maria. It wasn't fair. O'Hara and Corri
had left him with the baby. And he'd lost even that.
He remembered O'Hara pushing a bag at him and
telling him to run and him taking it and turning to run
and dashing slap into that tall guy out of the private
car. He'd put his head down to butt the interfering
bastard and then the next minute he was on the ground
with the guy on top. After that the cops had hold of him.
It wasn't fair. Of all the lousy outfits. And now this
unearthly quiet! He couldn't stand it! It was driving
him scatty! Hadn't they never heard of radio in these
places?

He dozed off when the lights went out but was woken
up a few hours later when the drunks began to arrive
in the other cells. He could have done with the quiet,
then. He was dog-tired. But they kept him awake; his
yells and curses joined theirs until morning.

After a frugal breakfast for which he had no appetite
he was ready to talk.

'O'Hara and Corri,' the detective-inspector said.
'Those their real names?'

'Your guess is as good as mine. First time I ever did a
job with them. Or this Len.'

'The one that didn't show up with the car?'

'I've told you, 'aven't I?'

'I like to check.' The inspector made a play of writing,
though a detective-sergeant was already taking down
the interview. He said, without looking up, 'And the
name of the man who fixed the job? What did you say
that was?'

'I didn't say.'

'What was the name you knew him by? Or weren't
you considered important enough to meet him?'

Ray's pride, already raw, was lacerated afresh.

'I met him all right. The fat, smooth—'

'Where did you meet him?'

'A pub.'

'What was his name?'

It went on like this for a long time, but in the end Ray gave in. His present experience was demoralizing him. He had so far got away with everything he attempted. He didn't count the times at the juvenile court when he had been put on probation and managed to escape being sent to Borstal, though he had spent some time at an approved school. He had always been a gang leader as a young boy; had won innumerable fights on account of his heavy physique. He had made himself feared; he had never been caught for his worst offences, because no one ever dared tell on him.

Of late years his luck had continued to hold. He had been noticed and picked out as a useful cosh. His pickings from the half-dozen or so jobs he had assisted at had been wealth to him, usually unemployed from sloth, stupidity or aggressiveness. These pickings would not have satisfied his associates but he did not realize that.

Now his entire world had collapsed and his self-confidence with it. He put his head down on the inspector's desk and sobbed like the childish, bullying booby he was.

'Pull yourself together,' said the inspector coldly. 'What was the name of the man who got you into this mess?'

'Mr. Burt,' sobbed Ray and continued to call down curses and threats on the head of his betrayer long after he was taken back to his cell.

The police were aware of the existence of the man, Burt. They rightly assumed that this was not his real name, but they were most anxious to trace him. The best way seemed to be through Ed, whom they could not hold. So they let him go and had him watched. He worked at the greengrocer's shop all day and then went to a pub in Notting Hill. But he spoke to no one and presently left and went to a block of flats where he also spent a few unproductive moments. After that he went home, still followed by his escort. It was the address he had given at the police station and his mother, tearful, complaining, stood up for him though quite obviously considering him fully guilty of whatever he was accused of. Ed, silent, sitting by the fire, did not turn his head during the short interview.

At the flats, later, Mr. Burt's door was opened by an overdressed, brightly painted artificial blonde, with a cigarette dangling from her lip.

'Mr. Burt? That's my landlord. No, he never comes here. Or hardly ever. Yes, it's my flat. Care to come in?'

The invitation was ambiguous and the officer declined it.

O'Hara and Corri were not names the Force was familiar with. On the other hand Len Smithson was. It took most of two days to pick up his trail from the grape-vine, but when they did trace him to Reading, his mother said he had been at home resting for the last week on account of a nasty cold. He had just taken a new job delivering cars and had gone up north.

'Can't say when he'll be back. Might switch to something else. You know Len.'

'I do indeed. He came down here last Friday, did he?'

'That's right.' She laughed, rather shakily. 'Now what am I saying? Friday week. On account of this cold. Friday week. About the middle of the afternoon. 'E looked awful.'

'I bet he did.'

Her interviewer reported that Len had undoubtedly gone straight to his mum, as they ought to have checked from the start. Would have checked, if they hadn't had that apparently first-hand information. Anyway his mum was very shaky on the alibi and he'd already left Reading. Probably back in London by now. Unless he'd really gone north, as she'd said. He did that as a rule if he thought the heat was on hard.

Meanwhile Belinda had written a long letter of explanation to her uncle, which crossed one from him expressing angry disappointment at her failure to carry out the simple mission he had given her to do for him. Since these letters took three days to arrive at their respective destinations, neither Belinda nor Sir John read them until Tuesday morning. Late on Saturday, however, the police received a message from Zürich, in reply to their own communication, asking them to instruct Miss Tollet to deal with the car forthwith.

'Who does he think he is?' grumbled the traffic police officer who was dealing with the affair. 'Can't he contact the girl herself?'

'Mean bloke, I should say,' his assistant answered. 'Wants to save the price of one wire.'

'They're all alike. Rolling in money and stingy as they come.'

Belinda got the message on Saturday evening when she reached her flat again, after spending the afternoon at Southfield. It rounded off a day of disagreeable surprises and experiences. The reason why she was back in the flat, instead of going on to spend the evening with Hugh was because they had quarrelled on the way home. Now there was this message, taken down hastily by one of her friends before the latter went out. The flat was empty, dark and cold. She found herself wishing she had asked Hugh in, quarrel or no quarrel. With tears pricking her eyes she lit the gas fire in the sitting-room the three of them shared and sat down to think things over.

First of all, this blasted car. She would have to get a garage to go down and change the wheel before she could drive it away. This would mean arranging with the police to open it, unless the key had been left in. Uncle John had left it in at the airport because he expected her to be there. The arrangement had been that she was to go straight to the car park at eight o'clock or as soon after as possible. He wanted to leave the key in the car in case she could not find him inside the airport buildings before he had to go out to the tarmac.

A crazy arrangement, really. No wonder it had been stolen. It was all very well for Hugh to say she ought to have made sure she would wake up, used an alarm clock or something, because of this about the key. It wasn't *her* Jag. If it had been she'd have left the key with someone responsible inside the buildings.

But it was no good binding over that point, now. The thing was how to fix it for the garage so that they could get at the spare wheel. In any case she couldn't do anything till Monday. No garage would undertake this job on a Sunday. It wasn't as if it was an emergency. Uncle John wouldn't want the Jag till Wednesday at the earliest. He would only get home on Tuesday evening.

She put the question of the car out of her mind. It would have to be dealt with on Monday, in her lunch hour, presumably. There wouldn't be any time before. Then she could go to the pound on Monday after work and drive down to Drews Court in it. Mrs. Heath would be expecting her.

'I was expecting you yesterday, miss,' Mrs. Heath had told her that afternoon. 'Sir John said to have a nice supper for you and get one of them from the Court to drive you down to the station afterwards.'

Mrs. Heath had been very worried when she didn't arrive, but she knew that Belinda occasionally kept the Jaguar for longer than was really intended.

'I haven't brought it back, now,' Belinda told her and explained what had happened.

'Oh dear,' Mrs. Heath said. 'I wonder what Sir John'll have to say to that.'

'I don't,' said Belinda, gloomily. 'I know only too darned well.'

She added, without much enthusiasm, 'Mr. Mellanby brought me down. He's over at Jeremy Ditchling's place. He's coming to pick me up when he's finished talking to Mr. Ditchling.'

'Mr. Ditchling was here on Thursday evening,' Mrs. Heath said. 'Called unexpectedly at about six. Sir John wasn't best pleased. I could see that. He must have left about an hour later, because when Mr. Mellanby came along about seven he'd just gone. I was in the kitchen getting the dinner started so I don't know the times exactly. Only I did hear Sir John saying, as they walked past the kitchen window that Mr. Ditchling had better take the footpath through the woods because that was the shortest way.'

Belinda nodded.

'I know. Hugh told me. But he wasn't there when he went back. Mr. Ditchling wasn't, I mean.'

Mrs. Heath's face took on a guarded look, but she only said, 'Poor Sir John. All his arrangements that evening went wrong. First Mr. Ditchling coming unexpected like, when we'd had no warning of it. Then Mr. Mellanby. And then Mrs. Wood getting down for dinner so early. He'd told me to make it nine, but she caught an earlier train and took a taxi from the station where he'd been going to meet her in the car. Saved him the journey, but he doesn't like his plans altered.'

No, thought Belinda now, still sitting staring at the gas fire which was burning her legs but did not seem to be warming the room at all. No, Uncle John, though the kindest of men, did like to have his own way and resented bitterly any of his plans going astray.

She had felt many guilty pangs while she was talking to Mrs. Heath. As the afternoon went on and there was still no sign of Hugh, the housekeeper had given her tea and continued to chat with her about local affairs.

'Mr. Ditchling isn't all that well thought of hereabouts,' she said. 'I hope you don't mind me saying that, miss?'

'I can't stand him, myself,' Belinda answered. 'I don't know what Hugh sees in him. Perhaps he's just sorry for him. He knew him at Oxbridge. He says he was very clever, then, but he went down without taking a degree.'

'Oh, he's clever all right,' said Mrs. Heath. 'But they wish he wasn't, up at the Court. Hangs about there a sight too much for Miss Pope's liking.'

Belinda nodded. This was just the sort of thing she expected to hear about Jeremy. A great shame. She wondered if Hugh knew the real reason for the horror coming to live at Southfield.

Drews Court, when it became in his view too expensive and too difficult to run, had been presented by Sir John to the government for use as an approved school for girls. This extremely generous offer had been accepted, though, being in the country and five miles from the nearest town, Southfield, there was some difficulty at first in securing staff. However, the authorities seemed to have got over this and to have kept it fully manned. The flow of inmates certainly never slackened from the day it opened.

By this philanthropic gesture Sir John increased his reputation for good works, chiefly among educationists and social workers. His chief interests had always been connected with the young. He had lost his wife early and had no children of his own. He was on the governing boards of several schools and was frequently on committees of various kinds connected with child welfare work and education. Drews Court approved school was his first venture into the delinquent side of juvenile activity.

Southfield and its surrounding countryside had not taken very kindly to Sir John's latest development. He had only lived there himself for about ten years. It wasn't as if he was a native or had any connection with the family that had originally built and owned the Court. He had simply bought the place because he had made a big fortune. In the country this did not carry with it the sort of respect his success brought him in urban or business circles. Also he had changed the name of the mansion from Southfield House to Drews

Court. This was considered ostentatious and slightly ridiculous. On the other hand the fact that he had transferred himself and many of his valuable possessions to the former lodge, now enlarged into a comfortable country cottage, had done much to restore confidence.

'If any of those youngsters want to steal they've got more at the lodge than any of us can offer,' was the general opinion.

But stealing was not the chief aberration for which the girls found themselves undergoing training, discipline, the rudiments of the education they had always ignored. A strong attempt was made to overcome their major obsession and direct their energies into more worthwhile channels.

'Men like this Mr. Ditchling are no sort of help to the girls we have up at the Court,' Mrs. Heath hinted.

It had been nearly six in the evening before Hugh drove up to the cottage to find Belinda. By this time she had exhausted all the usual topics of conversation with Mrs. Heath and was in a very bad temper. Hugh was also in a bad temper. More than that, he was obviously worried. They drove away in an angry silence. It was some minutes before Hugh spoke.

'Jeremy hasn't been seen since Thursday,' he explained. 'I don't believe he went back to the cottage after he left here, or perhaps just to pick up a bag, after I'd gone.'

'Mrs. Heath thinks he picked up the bad girls. To quite an extent, the rumour has it.'

'Oh. Well, that could account for delay, I suppose. But, damn it all, he was expecting me to dinner. It was his idea. But everything is exactly as it was when I was in the house on Thursday. Exactly. He can't have done more than gone in and out again. As far as I can see.'

'What d'you mean?'

'Well, the place is locked up. I could only look through the windows.'

'Why did he leave it unlocked before, when he was expecting you?'

Hugh hesitated. Then he said, 'Perhaps because he *was* expecting me'.

'If he did go away on Thursday, does it matter?'

'It matters a hell of a lot.'

'Can't you explain?'

'I'm afraid I can't. No, darling, I'd like to, but I can't. And I'm really scared.'

'For Pete's sake, what of?'

'Suicide.'

That startled her. She turned her head to look at him. His face in the dim light from the dashboard looked white and strained.

'Jeremy commit suicide! Impossible!'

His answer came, quick and furious.

'You don't know a darned thing about it, or him. You're so prejudiced—'

'All right. I don't know a darned thing. So tell me.'

There was no answer, though she waited for a long time. At last she said, 'Were you looking for him?'

'Yes.'

'Where?'

'In the woods behind his bungalow. Along the river for about a mile up and down from the bridge.'

She realized that he was taking this very seriously. It enraged her still further. Jeremy wasn't worth it. He was a slob, a louse, a low-down crook, probably.

'It doesn't occur to you that he may simply have tried to steal the Jag – to sell it, probably – and went off to hide up somewhere when he got the puncture?'

'Why attract attention by disappearing? The day before, too? Why not just go home, give me dinner and then go up to town? If he had any intention of stealing the Jag, which I doubt.'

'Because he happened to meet a delinquent miss?'

'But why stand me up? Drawing attention to himself? And why not just go home again, if he did take

43

the Jag? If the puncture happened to him, why not just go home after that?'

'Was that what you thought? You'd find he was back?'

Again no answer. Tension between them was at breaking point. When Belinda made a small but vindictive criticism of his driving, it snapped. The quarrel blazed suddenly and burnt itself out, leaving a sour ash.

So now Belinda sat miserably by her gas fire waiting for his telephone call, which never came. She went to bed early to avoid having to speak to the other two when they came back from their Saturday evening outings.

CHAPTER FIVE

THERE was no word from Hugh on Sunday and Belinda did not feel sufficiently anxious about their relationship to make the first move towards reconciliation. She fully intended to marry Hugh, but was quite aware that this idea had, as yet, not taken definite shape in his mind. It had only just taken definite shape in her own. Besides, he was in no position to marry. He had chosen what seemed to her a ludicrous gamble of a profession. It was no use Hugh telling her he was in the same position as a medical man aspiring to become a consultant. There was really no comparison. The medico, and she recalled a little wistfully a very attractive one, the last boy-friend before Hugh, who had explained to her all the bottlenecks of registrarship. He had become impatient himself and had emigrated, as so many others had, fed up with the inadequate salaries and prospects in the Health Service. But he had always said that most people, if they were reasonably gifted and persistent, got there in the end. In the law, it seemed to her, you could be brilliant and kick your heels for ever. There was no guarantee, no recognized progression, no certainty even that the whole market would not collapse. The money, after all, came mostly out of the pockets of the wealthy and they were an uncertain and variable community.

Sunday dragged slowly by. Belinda's only consolation was that it rained and there was no incentive to go out anyway. Also her two companions were quiet and listless after their activities of the evening before. So all three girls washed their clothes, wrote letters to their parents or friends and gossiped about their acquaintances. In the late afternoon, becoming suddenly bored, they went to the cinema together.

On Monday, Belinda, who had not slept well, woke early. She first of all decided to get to the office in good time so that she could make her arrangements about the Jag on the office phone. Then she realized that this might take rather a long time, so she decided to do her telephoning from the flat and perhaps be late at the office. That might mean telling her boss about her difficulties over the car, but he was a kind man and she did not anticipate any serious trouble with him. It was just the sort of story that would interest and amuse him, she thought.

The traffic department police at Scotland Yard were difficult. They kept putting her off and passing her on. It seemed to be impossible to find the man who had rung through a message on Saturday afternoon, while she was out.

In the end she was put in contact with someone who immediately attacked her for not getting in touch before and for not removing the car on Sunday.

'The garages were shut,' she explained.

'Did you try the A.A.? Sir John Drewson has the badge on the car.'

'No. I didn't. And I wouldn't have had the card. Also I haven't got the key. How would they open the boot to get out the spare if they couldn't get the boot key from the locker on the dashboard?'

This produced a dead silence followed by some rapid questions. But in the end a plan was worked out. Belinda was to get a garage to send a man to change the wheel in the pound, preferably Sir John's regular garage, referring authority to the police, if necessary. They would see that the mechanic had access to the spare wheel. She could then come down and remove it, subject to Sir John's written authority arriving in time.

All this took so long that Belinda had to rush off to the office without getting in touch with the garage. She did this, however, as soon as she was released for lunch, but found to her dismay that their mechanics were fully booked up for the whole afternoon. They could do the job the following afternoon if that would suit. Or she could get someone else to take it on. Belinda, daunted by the prospect of finding another garage, not knowing any, and forgetting once again that the A.A. could undoubtedly have helped her, closed with the offer. She explained where the car was and how the mechanic could get hold of the key. The garage promised, though now clearly with reluctance, to manage all this for Sir John.

After all, the manager said to the foreman later, Sir John was one of these V.I.P.s and even if he didn't very often bring the Jag in, he did occasionally park it with them for a night or two and paid well and promptly for service. Miss Tollet was in a flap over the business, as well she might be. It would be doing them both a good turn.

'I'll go down myself,' the foreman said. 'The boys wouldn't like asking those rozzers for the key and that.'

'Work it how you like, Sid,' the manager told him. 'Miss Tollet will be down there to collect by half past five, she says. So long as it's ready by then.'

On Tuesday morning Belinda got the promised letter from her uncle. There was anger in it and disappointment at her slackness and quite a lot of general criticism about the irresponsibility of modern youth and allied subjects. But at the end of the letter there was one piece of near satisfaction. The conference would end on Monday, as arranged, but he had been invited to visit some educational establishments in various parts of Switzerland and was postponing his return until Friday. He had already written to Mrs. Heath to warn her of this.

That meant she would not have to meet an irate uncle when she got down to Southfield that evening with the car. And she would be able to send him a wire to say it was safely at home again. By the time he returned his anger would have evaporated. Perhaps he would have forgiven her enough to ask her to Drews Court Cottage for the weekend. In which case she would go, unless Hugh wanted her to stay in town.

The thought of Hugh spread a small cloud on the clearing sky of her future. But it was nothing to the hideous storm that broke over her at four o'clock that afternoon.

At half past three, Sid, the foreman mechanic at Sir John's garage, arrived in a breakdown van at the pound. He produced a note from the garage manager which put the policeman on duty in the picture. Further explanations were needed about the car key, but the van was admitted and in due course moved as near as possible to the disabled Jaguar, which was by now hemmed in on all sides.

'Think you can manage?' asked the policeman who had gone with Sid to the spot.

'Reckon I'll have to. You going to open up for me?'

'That's the idea.'

The two men squeezed their way between the closely packed cars. When they reached the Jaguar Sid stooped to look at the flat tyre.

'Whoever got this lot didn't cotton on soon enough,' he said. 'Looks as if he'd driven it flat for a bit.'

'It was abandoned in a side road,' answered the other. 'Probably began to go down in the main road and he drove it off to be less noticeable.'

'He? I thought it was Drewson's niece? That Miss Tollet. She's the one that drives it around in London. The old boy only drives in the country, or so he says. Though he has brought it in at night himself to our place more than once. That I do know. We've an all-night service, see. And lock-ups. Mostly full of regulars, those.'

'I see. Well, as I understand it, Miss Tollet was not driving this time – or so she says. Sir John Drewson was in the air on his way to Switzerland where he still is.'

'Some people are always on the gad,' remarked Sid, sourly.

While this conversation was going on he had been taking down various tools from his van, a large jack, a wheel-brace and so on.

'O.K. mate,' he said, looking round.

The policeman opened the car door, took the boot key and stooped towards the boot. He now straightened himself, sniffing in a puzzled manner.

'What's up?' Sid asked.

He went closer. They both sniffed.

'Drains?' asked Sid.

'Whatever it is it's in the boot,' answered the officer. 'Shouldn't wonder if the old boy's been shooting down at his place in Sussex and forgotten to take his birds out of there.'

This officer had been brought up in the country, so his idea, at the end of October, seemed to him a natural one. Sid, London born and bred, was not impressed.

'Well, get on with it, whatever it is,' he urged. 'I got things to do back at the works.'

The boot opened upwards. The officer pushed it up, exclaimed 'My God!' and dropped it again with a bang.

'What's up?' Sid had been pulling forward the jack, not looking. He was astonished to see his companion's face grow white and then green.

'What's up?' he insisted. 'You look as if you'd seen a ghost.'

Being of lively intelligence and moreover impatient at the delay and the curious shocked immobility of the other, he pushed up the boot himself and saw the folded-up figure of a fully dressed man, his discoloured decomposing face half buried in a thick plaid rug.

Sid was a middle-aged man, a good many years older than the constable. He had fought in the Second World War and had been familiar with death, both recent and old. It was startling to come across it again in these quite different circumstances, but he took a firm grip on himself and secured the boot in an open position. Then he took another look at the corpse and anger flooded him.

'Why don't you do something?' he barked at the shaken officer. 'It's your job, isn't it? *Do* something! How the 'ell can I get at the spare wheel with *that* lying over it?'

This callous indifference helped the younger man more than any sympathy would have done.

'You'd better go straight back. You won't be able to change the wheel now. No one will be able to have this car for quite a time.'

'O.K.' said Sid, laconically. He began to trundle the jack back towards his van.

'Half a sec.' Routine began to assert itself. With an effort the policeman shut the boot and locked it. 'I'll have to ask you to wait till I've contacted my superior.'

'What the blazes for? You spotted the stiff yourself, didn't you? Nothing to do with me.'

'I must ask you to wait till I have further instructions.'

Sid looked at him contemptuously. No initiative. No guts. Not surprising, this crime increase, if all coppers were like this one.

He ostentatiously invited his companion into the van and drove him back to the entrance of the pound. While the latter settled down to the telephone he lit himself a cigarette and leaned against the van, smoking quietly. Presently the other came out to him.

'You can go,' he said. 'But keep this business under your hat for a couple of hours. We don't want a crowd round here till we've – well, anyway, keep your mouth shut till you see it in the papers. Right?'

'Have to mention it to the boss. He'll want to know why I been such a hell of a time doing damn-all.'

'O.K. But tell him what I've said. No general release till after you see it in the papers.'

In a very short time two plain-clothes men were at the pound. At ten minutes to five Belinda was called to the telephone at the office. A smooth voice addressed her.

'Miss Tollet?'

'Yes. Speaking.'

'This is Detective-Chief-Superintendent Mitchell's office at Scotland Yard. The superintendent would be obliged if you would call here to see him as soon as possible.'

'Me?'

'Yes, miss.'

'Whatever for?'

'In connection with Sir John Drewson's car, Jaguar, XYZ 2345.'

'He only has one, you know. But *why*? I'm going to fetch it away, starting *now*. It's all arranged.'

There was a slight pause, then the smooth voice continued. 'There has been an unforeseen development in connection with the car.'

'Can't they change the wheel? They were taking the dud back to the garage to mend it. Surely—'

'If you would prefer us to call for you, Miss Tollet, I shall be pleased to provide transport.'

'Good-oh. Only – look, tell your driver to wait a few doors down on the same side of the street, will you?'

She glanced round and dropped her voice.

'I wouldn't like my boss to think I was being arrested.'

'Very well, miss.'

'Hi! Wait! You don't know the address.'

'Yes, we do, Miss Tollet. In five minutes, then.'

Belinda put the receiver back slowly. She was puzzled, a little anxious. Scotland Yard itself. *What* could it be? At the same time she felt a wave of thankfulness when she remembered that Uncle John was not arriving back today. She had another forty-eight hours clear, at least.

Her boss, she found, when she was back at her desk, had already left. He had signed his letters. She only had to fix the envelopes, all ready and waiting and then she was free.

The police car was standing about twenty yards up the street. Belinda hurried to it, got in and was driven away.

At six o'clock she was back at the flat, ringing up Hugh Mellanby at his chambers. She got through at once.

'Hugh, darling?'

'Linda?'

'Yes. Something frightful has happened!'

'I think I know.'

'You can't. Darling, they've found a body in the boot of Uncle John's car. They think it's Jeremy Ditchling!'

CHAPTER SIX

Hugh's voice came slowly, painfully.

'They *know* it's Jeremy. At least there were things in the pockets that belonged to him. I've got to go along now to identify, I'm afraid. His people live in the north.'

'Oh, Hugh, how horrible for you!'

'It won't be pleasant.'

His voice was still quiet but she understood the strain

51

behind it. She said, anxiously, 'Darling, when you've done that come straight here, will you? I – I'm sorry I was such a pig the other day. Please come. I don't understand how this can have happened. I'm terrified.'

There was silence for several seconds. Then Hugh said, still in the same quiet, tense voice, 'Right, I'll be along,' and then he rang off.

It was two hours before he arrived at Belinda's flat. She had a stiff drink waiting for him and a carefully chosen meal to follow which she forced upon him immediately after he appeared to be reviving from his ordeal. Neither of them spoke about the actual identification, either then or at any time later. But she was surprised by Hugh's apparent lack of any kind of grief or even concern for his friend's fate. He was worried, more worried than ever before, but he was not sad.

'Couldn't the cops have got hold of his relations?' she asked, when they had settled down with coffee and brandy after the meal.

'I mean, couldn't they have waited, instead of picking on you to identify?'

'His parents live in Yorkshire,' he answered. 'The law wanted it done at once. He's been dead four days already. The pathologist wanted to get on with the job.'

She shuddered.

'I suppose so. Hugh, what did he die of? I mean, how was he killed? He must have been killed, mustn't he? But how did he get into Uncle John's car? It's a nightmare! I don't think – I —'

'Steady! There's no point asking me all those questions. Why didn't you ask them when you were at the Yard yourself?'

'I did. They wouldn't say a thing. Only asked me again exactly what I'd done or rather didn't do about collecting the Jag.'

'Nor did they tell me anything. But they wanted to know a hell of a lot about my going down to Southfield and not finding him there. And they wanted every last detail of what I did on Friday morning up to nine-thirty.'

'In case it was really you that took the Jag from the airport? Then they think whoever put Jeremy in the car did it that morning between stealing it and getting the puncture?'

'That would appear obvious, don't you think? The car was in your uncle's garage the night before.'

'D'you think they took the car to take the body away from somewhere? He couldn't have been killed at the airport, could he?'

'I shouldn't think so. But we don't know what killed him, yet.'

'Didn't you think the car had been stolen to act as a getaway in that wages snatch?'

'Did I?'

'You said so.'

She stared at him. He looked very strange, still paler than she had ever seen him and in spite of his evident self-control, strained nearly to breaking point.

She could not help herself. She burst out, 'I must say you don't seem to care very much that he's dead. I thought he was a real, important friend of yours.'

'No.'

The answer came in a low voice, almost a whisper.

'Then *why* did you go down to see him – *twice*? Why spend all that time looking for him? Or wasn't it Jeremy you wanted at his house? Was it something else you'd gone down for?'

Hugh turned his head away from her so that she could not see his face. But his words were disturbing enough.

'It's no use asking me questions, Linda. I can't tell you the answers. I can't tell you anything.'

She did not try to press him any further. Not because his attitude made her angry, but because she was too frightened. She realized that she did not really know Hugh very well. They had gone about together for three months now. They had indulged in some not very advanced love-making. She knew that he had to work hard at this stage of his career and was content to let their relationship develop slowly. This extraordinary and quite horrible event had shown her how deep her love for him had grown and at the same time how narrow as yet was the base of their friendship. When, after a long silence, he got up and said he must go home she did not try to stop him. She only said, 'When do you think they'll let me have the Jag?'

'I should think when they've gone over every inch of it with a high-powered lens they'll take it back to Drews Court themselves. They're sure to want to talk to Sir John about the whole affair.'

'Why? He's been away all the time.'

'Why? Because he seems to have been the last person to see Jeremy alive, doesn't he?'

As he left the flat the unworthy thought flashed into her mind that he had rather laboured this point. Was Uncle John *really* the last person to see Jeremy alive, or had Hugh perhaps— But no, of course not. Neither of them. The last person to see Jeremy alive was the man who had killed him and put him in the boot of Uncle John's car.

Hugh turned away from the flat and walked all the way back to his lodgings, trying to sort out what he knew from what he had told the police. Not that he had told them lies. He had described exactly, but not quite fully, all his movements on Thursday when he had gone to Southfield at Ditchling's invitation and his subsequent movements on Saturday when Belinda had driven down with him but had walked on from the bungalow without even going inside the garden gate.

He must always remember, he told himself, he had said that on this occasion the bungalow door had been locked, whereas on Thursday it was open and he had left it open, after going inside to look for his host. This had seemed to interest Detective-Chief-Superintendent Mitchell.

'You knew him well enough to look round his house

when he was not there?' the superintendent had asked.

'Well, yes.'

Hugh described his early knowledge of Jeremy Ditchling, both at Oxbridge and subsequently in London.

'Then you are aware of the reason for his being sent down in his third year?'

'No.'

This was true, though Hugh had guessed it since. He realized that the police probably knew also, which made it more important than ever for him to watch his step.

'No. It was very much hushed up and in any case by that time I was seeing very little of him. We had developed quite different circles of friends.'

'That doesn't surprise me.'

The superintendent considered for a few seconds. Here was a young man who was cool, if somewhat shaken by his trying ordeal. If he had anything to hide he was capable of keeping it hidden very thoroughly. Also he was a barrister with the powerful support of his profession behind him. Also, if he was as completely on the level as he made himself out to be, he could be useful. Mitchell decided to test the young man's apparent strength with a quick jolt.

'You realize we have already begun to investigate this affair at Mr. Ditchling's bungalow, don't you?'

'Obviously.'

'We have been taking photographs and looking for fingerprints and so on. Did you touch anything by any chance while you were inside the place?'

The answer came with no hesitation at all.

'Of course. The front-door handle, the other door handles one by one.' Hugh frowned, remembering and deciding it was safe to continue. 'The table in the sitting-room. I moved a few books on it. I was looking for a written message to say why he was out.'

'But you did not find one?'

'No. I looked in the bureau, too. Again, no message.'

'Wasn't that rather – well – cheek? At least, unusual. To pry into another man's private desk?'

Hugh flushed at the tone of the other's voice, but he answered quite steadily.

'I don't think so. It wasn't locked. I expected it to be locked, as a matter of fact.'

'Then why did you try it?'

The question came with lightning swiftness. Careful, thought Hugh. This man is dangerous.

'Still looking for a message. Jeremy was always a queer bird. He might have left a scribbled note of some sort – almost anywhere – he did that sort of thing at college when we knew each other fairly well. But there was nothing. One or two papers in the bureau but nothing for me.'

'Did you go through the papers to establish that?'

'No. Why should I? A message would have been left on top, wouldn't it?'

'I have no idea.' Mitchell paused, then went on smoothly, 'Mr. Mellanby, have you any objection to giving us your fingerprints?'

Mitchell watched the young man's eyebrows go up, but the quick surprise was not followed by any other emotion.

'Well, no. I suppose you want to eliminate all mine from the bungalow. There must be quite a few scattered over it.'

'We would like to identify them,' the superintendent corrected.

Hugh grinned at him. He was not in the least perturbed. 'Go ahead,' he said. 'Anything to help.'

Mitchell had not become any more affable but he had asked no more questions.

When Hugh reached his own room after leaving Belinda, he first locked the door. Then, putting on the reading lamp which stood on a small table under the window he sat down to examine once more a photograph he had studied at intervals during the last four days. It was the photograph of a girl in a room. There was some vague furniture behind her, blurred and out of focus. A man, his back to the camera and his whole figure in shadow, was leaning a little forward as she was leaning back. His hands gripped her bare shoulders, his head was thrust forward apparently reaching for her mouth. The light fell on her face, making her quite recognizable to anyone who knew her. The same could not be said of the man; his features were hidden but his build was clearly defined. His head was in shadow, merging with the shadow that fell half across his body.

Hugh stared at this photograph and then at the envelope from which he had taken it and which he had found lying inside the bureau at the bungalow. The envelope was not sealed. It was of postcard size, like the photograph. The flap had merely been tucked in. There was no name on it, no address. Instead, in pencil, in large writing, there was written '£500' with a firm sloping line drawn underneath.

'He was crazy,' Hugh thought, putting the envelope back in his wallet, from which he had taken it. 'Stark, staring, raving—'

He sat down heavily, wondering what his next move ought to be.

*　　*　　*

The forensic pathologist, who had the unpleasant duty of examining the remains of Jeremy Ditchling, found that the young man had died partly from suffocation, but chiefly from an overdose of a barbiturate drug. A search of the bungalow had not revealed any of the same type of barbiturate, though various little packets and tubes of tablets proved to be sedatives and tranquillizers of different makes.

Nothing much was discovered on his person or in his house to throw any light on his activities. He had a few notes in his wallet, a few coins in his trouser-pocket. A bunch of keys included those of the bungalow front and back doors, but did not fit anything else in or about the house. One letter in his inside breast pocket, written by

Hugh Mellanby, confirmed that the latter had in truth gone down in response to an invitation from the dead man. No other letters of any kind were found at the bungalow. The desk contained a few manuscript articles for newspapers, a few ordnance survey maps of southern counties, some writing materials and postage stamps.

'Either he made no mark on the place, no personal mark, I mean,' Superintendent Mitchell said at South-field police station, 'or someone has been round it, clearing up.'

'But there weren't many fingerprints, other than his own, were there?' said the local detective-inspector.

'No. A fair number of Mellanby's. One or two of another individual's. Incidentally several of those on the desk lid and inside the bureau are Mellanby's and a few small ones that look like a girl's. If we've got those in our records it's a fair guess the owner is in residence at Drews Court. You say Ditchling was thought to be running after one of the girls from there?'

'Nothing proved. He certainly hung about the place to some extent, but so do a fair number of our local lads. Miss Pope does wonders with most of the girls but there are always a few hard cases that give trouble.'

'I'll have a word with her if we turn up any of her charges.'

'There's one thing defeats me,' said the inspector. 'Mr. Mellanby says he found the bungalow unlocked the first day he went down. The day he was invited for. He says he went in, had a look round and not finding anyone went on to see Sir John. Later he went back to the bungalow which was still unlocked and still empty. But two days later, when he went down again with Miss Tollet, the doors were locked, back and front and all the windows shut, too. Now I've made extensive inquiries here and all round, but no one local that I can find went anywhere near the bungalow between Thursday evening and Saturday afternoon. So who locked those doors?'

'What about the milkman?' asked Mitchell.

The inspector smiled.

'Ditchling fetched his milk from the farm, a bit farther up Neots Lane. He was so uncertain about when he was going to be down and for how long, the farmer refused to call. Didn't like seeing his good milk standing on the doorstep, going sour, even if Mr. Ditchling did pay for it later. So he told him to go up to the farm himself, whenever he wanted any.'

'I see. The same with the other tradesmen, I suppose?'

'That's right. The place is a bit out of the way, like.'

'I quite agree. It's an interesting point about the doors. It's been worrying me quite a bit. Whoever locked up left no prints and that's suggestive apart from the question of whether anything was taken.'

'Always supposing Mr. Mellanby is speaking the truth.'

'I think he may be about the doors. He's unlikely to have duplicate keys to the bungalow and Ditchling's set was in his pocket.'

'Yes, of course.'

'I think Mellanby's speaking the truth,' said Mitchell, 'but I'm pretty sure it's not the whole truth.'

In London Sir John Drewson's Jaguar was very thoroughly searched, both the boot and the inside of the car. The butt of a cigarette of the brand represented by the carton the police constable had found lying on the road in Fulham was picked up from under the driver's seat. There were several fingerprints about the car both inside and out, but none of these corresponded with any in the records. Certainly not with Len Smithson's. Neither the boot nor the inside of the car contained an object for which a very special search was being made. This was a button from the dead man's jacket. His clothes were in good condition, though creased and superficially soiled. But the top button of the jacket was missing.

'It seems fairly clear,' Mitchell remarked to

Detective-Sergeant Jones, when they were back at the Yard after seeing the Jag, 'that he was bundled into the boot when he was unconscious or dead. The button could have caught on something and been dragged off. I thought we might have found it in the boot.'

'Wasn't he suffocated in there?' asked the sergeant.

'Not necessarily. We don't know where or when he was drugged. He could have been hidden in a cupboard or wardrobe or anything like that just as well as the boot of the car. He may even have taken the drug himself and then an enemy took advantage of his condition. Perhaps he was hidden in some enclosed space and transferred to the car later. We can't speculate profitably.'

'I thought Dr. Wing gave the time of death as Friday morning?'

'He wasn't sure. Depends if the car was warm from running, after Ditchling was put into it. And whether he was alive then or not. If the car was warm that might hurry up decomposition after he died. If he was kept in a cold place, dead, before being put in the boot the death could have been earlier. It's impossible to say.'

'It couldn't have been earlier than Thursday evening, could it? He left Sir John's cottage between six and seven.'

'Quite. On the other hand if he was doped and put in any cold airless place and then transferred to the boot on Friday morning, we should get the picture we have.'

'He must have been put in the Jag, then, between an unknown time after eight, when the car was parked at London airport, and nine-thirty or so when it was abandoned in Fulham.'

'That's right. We've got to find out two things. Who took that car and when. And who were Jeremy Ditchling's friends. I'm seeing the parents this afternoon. The inquest's tomorrow, but it'll be adjourned.'

The Ditchling couple, very simple, ordinary Yorkshire townspeople, who owned a small shop, could not supply any recent news of their son, their only child. They had always been bewildered by his precocious intelligence, proud of his record at school and the scholarship that gave him his place at the university, but quite unable to help him to find his feet there, and shocked, horrified and more than ever confused by his later development, which they never spoke about.

They had managed to find a photograph of him taken two years before, when he had been engaged to be married to a local girl. That had been another disappointment.

'He was not actually married, was he?' Mitchell asked.

'No,' Mrs. Ditchling answered sadly. 'We thought he treated her very badly. Went off to London and didn't write for six months. And then only to say it was finished as far as he was concerned. She took it very hard.'

'I don't blame her,' said Mitchell. 'Do you?'

'Oh, no,' Mrs. Ditchling agreed. 'You couldn't blame her.'

'That wasn't the only time he behaved badly, was it?' Mitchell went on. 'What about his college career?'

Mr. Ditchling drew himself up.

'My son is dead,' he said, with dignity, 'I'm not going to have aspersions cast on him now.'

Looking at his lined, grief-stricken face and remembering Mellanby's vagueness on the same subject, Superintendent Mitchell wondered if Mr. Ditchling and his wife were equally ignorant, or wished to be thought ignorant, of the cause of Jeremy's undergraduate failure.

CHAPTER SEVEN

LEN SMITHSON, working for a firm of road hauliers based on Warrington in Lancashire, read the accounts of Jeremy Ditchling's death with very mixed feelings. He was pleased to be so far from the scene of police operations and congratulated himself upon the smoothness with which his plans had worked out. He was not surprised to learn that the man whom he had known as Jimmy Dice turned out to have this posh name, Jeremy Ditchling. He had never thought Dice was his real name. No one with any sense in his loaf would use his own name for the sort of thing Jimmy had been up to.

Everything, he decided, had worked out for the best, except for that early, almost catastrophic puncture in Fulham. But a letter from his mother addressed to him at a small post office in Wigan, that he was in the habit of using as an accommodation address when he worked in the Manchester area, had bothered him a good deal. She had mentioned a visit from the police and though he knew he could rely on her not to mention place-names he was pretty certain she would have told them that he had changed his job and gone up north. Because this was what he usually did when the heat was on in London. It would never have occurred to him to change his tactics, his carefully worked out routine.

But it bothered him to know that the rozzers had already called at his mother's home in Reading. It meant that someone had squealed. Must have. Probably that young larrikin, Ray. He hadn't much use for Ray. The boy looked tough but he was soft inside. He'd warned Mr. Burt not to include Ray in the team, but the boss was not a man you could tell. He'd just smile in that nasty way he had and tell you to mind your own business.

When, a couple of days later, a fuller story appeared

in the papers, together with the photo of Jeremy Ditchling provided by his parents, Len became very worried indeed. There was this appeal for friends or acquaintances of the dead man. There was a full description of the outside of his bungalow in its secluded spot up Neots Lane, five miles from Southfield town and a mile and a half from Sir John Drewson's cottage, near the main road at the entrance to Drews Court approved school for girls. There was no doubt in the minds of the journalists that the young man had been murdered, though by what means and why and how his body came to be in Sir John's abandoned car was being worked up in the papers into a really first-rate mystery and horror story. Which Len found definitely disturbing.

The inquest had been called and adjourned for a week after identification of the remains. Len had never heard of Hugh Mellanby, the young barrister who had first named the discovered corpse. The father had also identified his son. The medical evidence was not taken; it was understood that various tests were still being made.

Altogether an unsatisfactory state of affairs from Len's point of view. The whole thing was beginning to get on his nerves. He was afraid it might soon affect his driving. Mostly he was taking a heavy lorry up to Carlisle and back. He began to find the hazards of Shap Fell getting him down. It was difficult to concentrate. At any time while he was thundering along the M6, or grinding his way up the hills beyond, a vision of Jimmy Dice's weak good-looking face would rise between him and the road. It was bad enough to think of the dead man curled up in the boot of the car he himself had driven. It was worse to remember that face leering at him, conscious of power, while he knew he couldn't even bash it in as it deserved.

Several times since he first read about Jimmy's fate Len had nearly come to grief on the road. By Thursday morning he decided to ask for his cards. He had made

up his mind what to do. On the same afternoon he
travelled by train to Fleetwood and took the night
boat to Belfast. By Saturday morning he was over the
border and no longer on British soil. In another two
days he had found himself a job with a hire-car firm in
Dublin. He had worked for them before, off and on.
They never asked any questions. He drove well and
gave no trouble at all and they could trust him not to
cheat over fares. Indeed it never occurred to him to
indulge in minor dishonesty. He was too much accustomed to the big jobs to bother himself with chicken-
feed.

In London the newspapers caused even greater
concern to O'Hara and Corri. They also recognized
the photograph of Jeremy Ditchling, whom they had
met occasionally as Jimmy Dice.

'Him as Len brought along, wasn't it?' O'Hara
asked, when he met Corri on the evening the full
details broke.

'That's right. But I rumbled the connection.'

'Jimmy worked for Mr. Burt. I know that. Len said
so.'

Corri muttered a curse on Mr. Burt's head.

'See 'im lately? I been at the flat twice. That floosie
said not ever come again.'

' 'E covers up very nice and snug,' O'Hara said.
'I'd give a lot to know where he really lives. But the
flat's got two entrances. 'E can just mark which one
you're at and go by the other. I've tried switching back
and forward but I never got to trail 'im yet.'

'Nor even to take 'is car number,' Corri added,
gloomily. 'If 'e 'as a car. Hire job, that's 'ow 'e operate.
No chance to pick up 'is own car if we can't never
follow. Not even know 'is proper name.'

'Think the skirt knows?'

'Nobody doesn't know. Why do we work for 'im?
Answer me that.'

O'Hara finished the beer in his mug and got up to
go to the bar for more. When he got back he said, as

if there had been no break in the conversation, 'Work for Mr. Burt? Because 'e gives a good percentage. That's why. Pays 'im and pays us. You know it as well as I do.'

O'Hara had been drinking steadily since the pub opened. He always drank hard when he was worried and just now he was a very worried man indeed, because the aftermath of the broken raid seemed to be piling up in a more than menacing way. O'Hara was feeling much more confident now than when he had arrived earlier in the evening. Consequently his voice had begun to rise a little above its normal careful hoarse whisper. Its tones had carried beyond Corri's ears to those of a small elderly man sitting at the next little round table to that occupied by Mr. Burt's henchmen.

This part of the pub, being in one of the corners farthest from the bar and nearest to the double half-glassed doors was chiefly in shadow. The small man did not look round but he edged a few inches nearer to Corri, while continuing to sip his pint and study his much-rolled newspaper. If O'Hara continued to spill when he came back from the bar, his evening might turn out to be profitable. He could do with that. The recent weeks had been lean ones.

O'Hara, with yet another full mug before him, was not only loquacious but belligerent.

'I've a good mind to turn up Mr. Bloody Burt for good an all,' he said, as he sat down.

'If 'e 'as not already turn us up,' said Corri. 'Looks like 'e don't want us no more.'

' 'E'd be bound to lay off a bit, stands to reason,' O'Hara argued. 'Don't make no mistake. I quit 'im, *if* I quit. The other way round don't make.'

Corri glanced about him nervously.

'Nark it!' he warned. 'No need to advertise. Mr. Burt 'e know everything. 'E know Len work with Jimmy. 'E know we know Len. Maybe 'e no want us work for 'im now.'

'It wouldn't surprise me,' O'Hara said, truculently,

'if Jimmy didn't work for Mr. Burt, too. That place down near Southfield belongs to Burt. You knew that, didn't you?'

Corri shook his head, finished his beer, wiped his mouth with the back of his hand and got up to go.

'You talk too much and too big,' he said, sharply, and went out through the double doors. He had decided to avoid all his regular haunts for the next few weeks. O'Hara, in his present mood, was a danger to his friends.

The London-bred Irishman sat on, sobered a little by Corri's last remark, glowering at the surrounding company that he had suddenly begun to hate. He would have been delighted, at that moment, to get into a scrap with anyone who happened to jolt his table, trip over his big feet, thrust out in front of him, or address him disparagingly. But no one took the slightest notice of him. The barman had slipped the word to one or two regulars that O'Hara was ready to turn nasty and the regulars knew just how nasty he could get.

Presently, bored with the silence and affronted by his companions' total neglect, O'Hara got up and followed Corri through the door. He was annoyed, when he reached the pavement and stood breathing deeply the cold damp night air, to find that Corri was not waiting for him. But the street was empty, there was no one at all upon whom he could vent his rage, his growing anxiety, his general discontent. So he went away, cursing under his breath, pronouncing revenge he knew he could not achieve on Mr. Burt, on Len, on the world in general.

After about ten minutes the small elderly man passed unnoticed through the pub door and after looking carefully up and down the street, made his way to a bus-stop and travelled about a mile farther north-west. He then found a public telephone and dialled Whitehall 1212, asking, when the connection was made, for Detective-Chief-Superintendent Mitchell. Detective-Sergeant Jones answered him and agreed to hear what the old man had to say. An appointment was fixed for the following morning, the informer handed over his news and received his pay.

'That might be useful, mightn't it?' Jones said, reporting to Mitchell. 'It explains how Ditchling came to be living down at Southfield.'

'Because the bungalow belongs to this man, Burt? Well, I never did think Ditchling bought it or hired it himself. So far the local chaps haven't turned up any estate agent who has handled the bungalow at any time. But they're working on it. All the same, Ditchling didn't live there simply because he knew Burt, whoever he may be, and accepted his kindness as a gift. He was playing some game of his own down there.'

'Wasn't he by way of writing a novel or something?'

'He gave that out in the neighbourhood. There is no trace of a manuscript. Only a few newspaper articles, unfinished.'

'Could the novel have been stolen?'

'Possibly. I doubt it. It wouldn't be worth anything, I shouldn't think. No. I believe Ditchling was working for Burt *and* for himself. With his early history we can guess roughly what at. Petty breakings and snitching small valuables. It's the right sort of neighbourhood. He was quite a presentable lad; with a bit more brains and guts he'd have made a first-class con man. But he hadn't got what it takes. In that direction, anyway. I'm sure we've got to follow that lead. And I think it takes us back to Hugh Mellanby, though just how it works beats me at present.'

*   *   *

Mr. Burt, so much discussed in his criminal circle and among the police, was, in his daily occupation, at the headquarters of a large insurance company in the City of London, not in the least prominent and not very highly regarded. He took care that this should be so. In his real name, Simpkins, he had a reputation for cold reserve, moderate ability, faithful attendance. But he had been several times passed over in the promotion scramble and this was as much deliberate policy on his own part as deliberate neglect by his employers. Mr. Burt and one or two other aliases he used had substantial, growing bank accounts and investments in various parts of the country and also outside it. Very soon, in a year or two, he thought, it might be possible for him to retire, take himself and a companion, perhaps his wife, perhaps Doll, or if more convenient just himself, to some foreign land and there enjoy the fruits of all his hard work and brilliant financial operations. In the meantime he must keep up his present character of dull, ordinary respectability. His little suburban house was run carefully at the fourteen-pounds-a-week level. The flat was showing a small profit. Florrie, no doubt, was cheating him in this. But she was a good girl; she could charge high fees and she was always glad to see him. She never made a fuss when he wanted the flat for conferences. She never pestered him with questions about his widely various operations.

But the Jimmy Dice affair had given him a most unpleasant jolt. It was bad enough to have Len mixed up in it, particularly as the latter had disappeared. Ireland again, he had no doubt. It was worse to have that particular car brought into such unexpected prominence. Far too many threads cut and hanging loose for the cops to pick up. Far too many disappointed men looking to him for satisfaction and not finding it. Florrie said they had been calling – the rozzers, too. That meant 'grass'. One of the new layabouts – Ray, he'd say, for a guess. He'd be for Borstal, most likely, but he might have done some damage all the same. Obviously he'd put Them on to the flat. But it wouldn't do to move. Florrie would have to stay, in her own interests, if not in his. It hurt him to think he would have to forgo his dividend on her earnings, but he wouldn't dare visit the place until well after the inquest. Much too risky.

In the train, for he never used his own car, registered

under his own name, except for weekend outings with his wife, Mr. Burt held his newspaper to his eyes, but he seldom turned the pages, for he was not reading the news. His eyes were turned inwards, seeing many disturbing scenes; particularly the visit he had paid to the bungalow at Neots Lane on the Saturday after the failed raid.

He had gone down, as usual, in a hired car, which he had left outside a farmhouse about a mile away, not far from the bridge over the river. He had walked up through the woods, where the path came out at an angle with Neots Lane about twenty yards from the bungalow.

He went in by the back door, using his own key. This was standard form, though he usually went at night, not in the early afternoon, as now. But with the failed raid to bother him he had decided to come down and collect. Even to himself he described his operations in this way. He had imagination. Schemes flashed into his mind. He organized, planned, blue-printed, financed. Success followed. And then he would pay off and collect.

But on that Saturday afternoon there was nothing for him. Again there was nothing, and this time no explanation, either. The house was empty. Far from collecting, the very assets to be used in the transaction had disappeared. Altogether. On the last occasion he had made only a cursory search. He had been sure of success later. But no, there was nothing.

This had given him a serious shock. But it was nothing to the fright he had a little later, when he was searching carefully through Jimmy's clothes. He heard a car draw up in the road and moved to the window. A man and a girl got out. He heard their voices distinctly.

She said, 'I don't want to meet him. I'll go on to the cottage. I have a few messages for Mrs. Heath.'

And he answered, 'O.K. I won't be very long. The place still looks deserted. Jeremy probably never came back. Can't think what he's playing at. At least—'

He did not finish because the girl turned away and walked off. In any case Mr. Burt did not wait. He was flying first to the front door and then to the back to make sure the former was locked and to fasten the one he had come in by. The front door was not locked. It made him sweat to think the contents of the house had been available to any chance passer-by. He crouched down just inside the back door. No one could see him there from the outside of the bungalow and if this chap, whoever he was, broke in, he himself could make a quick and practically silent getaway into the woods.

But the visitor did not break in. He rattled the doors and knocked, and rang the bell and shouted 'Jeremy!' several times, but after a while he went away and still later Mr. Burt heard the car start up and move off. He did not wait long after that to leave the bungalow himself. He locked the back door again after fastening the catch on the front yale. He had his own set of keys because the bungalow belonged to him. Before he left he had another look for Jimmy's keys but failed to find them anywhere.

Driving home and frequently during the days that followed, increasingly often after Jimmy Dice, whose real name turned out to be Jeremy Ditchling, had turned up, dead, Mr. Burt pondered over the words he had heard the unknown man say outside the bungalow. 'The place still looks deserted. He probably never came back.'

So the visitor had been there before. When? And for what purpose? Was he this Hugh Mellanby whose name was in the papers? Hugh Mellanby, the barrister, or that other chap, Bob Low, his friend? And why was Jimmy out when he called -- that first time! Well, that was obvious. He knew exactly what Jimmy had been up to, the dirty twister.

Two things were abundantly clear. Jimmy had been running sidelines, as he had often suspected. And Jimmy had welched. What had begun to worry Mr. Burt more and more seriously was the thought that a number of persons unknown to him had been closely concerned with a man he had thought he controlled, but quite evidently had not. The whole situation was infuriating. And not only that. It was too late now to get at the exact truth. Somewhere along the line he himself had slipped up. Deep in his heart Mr. Burt knew that he was afraid.

CHAPTER EIGHT

By Friday, the day on which Sir John Drewson was due to arrive back in England, Superintendent Mitchell, with several reports on his desk, was in a position to review the case of 'the body in the boot' as the Press now called it. But he had made uncomfortably little progress.

Dr. Wing, the pathologist, was in his office.

'You found a lethal dose of the barbiturate in his body, I see, doctor,' Mitchell said.

'We did. He would have died in any case.'

'And we know, from some of his more forthcoming associates, that he took a variety of drugs,' Mitchell added. 'You can't tell us when the fatal dose was taken?'

'Not the date and time. It was taken about three hours before death, and the death was accelerated by partial asphyxia.'

'Yes. Well, we must hope to get a clearer line on the date later on. Sir John may be able to help us there. No clues from the stomach contents as to time, I suppose?'

'The stomach was practically empty of food content.'

'Which is what you'd expect if he'd gone straight back to London after leaving Drews Cottage without seeing Mellanby and if he'd been drugged either that evening before having a meal or the next morning before breakfast.'

'I thought you said Ditchling was a man of irregular habits. If he drugged he wouldn't be likely to have regular meal-times. Or indeed eat proper meals at all.'

'That's true. And it doesn't make our job any easier.'

Dr. Wing got up.

'Sorry I can't be more definite. It's a pity they didn't think of jacking up that wheel in the pound. Better for the car and they'd have found the body three days earlier. It must have occurred to them an owner wouldn't have just abandoned it.'

'You've no idea the fool things owners get up to.' said Mitchell. 'It might have been just a misunderstanding. As it nearly was in this case. The girl Tollet failed to go for it and asked her boy-friend to do so. He found it gone and concluded she'd gone after all and not let him know.'

'But if either of them had got the puncture they'd have taken steps, wouldn't they?'

'I suppose so. But the chaps at the pound aren't there to look after the cars. They're teaching a lesson to owners, or trying to.'

Dr. Wing went towards the door.

'Any idea when you'll be ready for the inquest?' he asked.

'None,' answered Mitchell, cheerfully. 'But I'll let you know in good time.'

Dr. Wing nodded and went away.

Looking down at the other reports before him Mitchell frowned. Progress was indeed miserably slow and much too diffused. Len Smithson, for instance. The superintendent was fairly certain that Len had stolen the Jaguar, and that he had been briefed to act with it as the getaway from the failed raid. This explained the failure, made certain by the worthy civilian who had blocked the villains' van, thus cutting off their alternative means of escape. It also explained the presence of the abandoned Humber in Wandsworth, near the tobacconist's shop, whose proprietor remembered a man buying cigarettes of the brand traces of which were found in both cars.

It was reasonable to suppose that Len had done nothing about the puncture in the Jag's tyre because there was no time if he was to perform his allotted task in the raid. But it was also possible that he could not open the boot to get out the spare wheel because he knew what was there as well. Sir John had left the car at the airport at eight or just after. The disabled Jaguar had been parked between nine-thirty and ten. It did not take, or it need not take, with the new Hammersmith flyover, an hour and a quarter to reach Fulham, even in the morning rush hour. The rush was worst between nine and ten, not between eight and nine. So Len might have gone somewhere to pick up the body. If so, where and why?

'Len knew him, that's certain,' Sergeant Jones reported in person. 'It points to him, doesn't it, sir, the way he's scarpered?'

Mitchell turned up another report.

'Crossed to Northern Ireland from Fleetwood yesterday afternoon. If I know him he'll be over the border into Eire by the end of the week. I agree it's suspicious. We've got to find out more detail of his connection with Jimmy Dice – Ditchling, we'd better call him from now on. What made him leave England? Just after the story broke in the papers, too? Work on that. How well did Ditchling know Len? Was he on to something Len didn't want known? Apart from these jobs he was doing from time to time?'

'Jimmy couldn't be this Mr. Burt, could he? I mean, Burt's not been seen or heard of at that flat since the day of the raid. There's been nothing on him at all, has there?'

'Nothing. But I don't believe Ditchling was capable of running a gang. Certainly not of planning a big scale raid. He was essentially weak; mean enough for his lying and small-time frauds, like the nasty little job that got him sent away from Oxbridge. But you can't imagine him working out a real blue-print for a big snatch, can you?'

'Not really.'

'Well, stick at it,' Mitchell told him. 'I'll get Interpol to locate Len in the Emerald Isle. It shouldn't be difficult. He usually works in Dublin when he goes to ground.'

The superintendent was certainly less interested in Len Smithson, with whose unvarying behaviour he was entirely familiar, than he was in Hugh Mellanby, an antagonist, if he proved to be one, of quite a different order. Mellanby's story was innocent enough, taken at its face value. He had been quite open about going into the bungalow on the Thursday evening. Evidence for this visit was supplied by Ditchling's papers. It was also possible that he had not been able to get into the bungalow again on the Saturday because it was locked up. But the second visit ought to mean he had been looking for something he had failed to find the first time. Very well. Either he couldn't get in and someone had forestalled him, locking the bungalow as he left, or else Mellanby did get in to search again and locked the place up after finding, or perhaps failing to find, what he sought. There had been nothing anyone could have wanted when the police searched the bungalow after Ditchling's body had been found.

So the next question was, if Mellanby didn't find anything the first time, could this be because Ditchling had it with him? The obvious reason for Mellanby's visit was, apart from the very unlikely, purely social one, blackmail. But which way round? The superintendent had to acknowledge that he hadn't the faintest idea. But the obvious thing was to have another go at the young barrister. Hugh made no objection to this and the same afternoon found him sitting with Mitchell, wary but obviously unafraid.

'I've asked you to come along again, Mr. Mellanby,'

the superintendent began, in an amiable voice, 'because I don't think you've been entirely frank with me.'

'Indeed?' answered Hugh, politely. 'In what way?'

'I want you to tell me what you were looking for at the bungalow and what, if anything, you found.'

'But I've told you already. A message which wasn't there.'

'On Saturday as well as Thursday?'

'Well, no. A message on Thursday. On Saturday I wanted to see Jeremy himself and get an explanation.'

'What of?'

'Not being there to give me dinner on Thursday, after he'd invited me down.'

It did not sound very convincing to Hugh as he said it. Looking at Mitchell he saw complete unbelief in the alert face opposite.

'You know that won't do, Mr. Mellanby. It simply won't do.'

Hugh kept his head, remembering his profession and using one of the basic tricks of his trade.

'What would you suggest instead, then?'

To his surprise Mitchell fell for this gambit, but as he proceeded Hugh realized that he must admit defeat, though he was still determined not to do so openly.

'I'll tell you,' the superintendent began. 'When Ditchling was up at Oxbridge he took to helping himself now and then to small sums of money that he found lying about and to cashing in on the odd camera or watch he managed to pick up without the owner noticing. He needed money to pay his debts because he had got in with a rather reckless card-playing clique and not being an adept always lost heavily. He didn't like to come down on his family for extra money. Now one of Ditchling's friends, also in the clique and in the same college, was another weak individual who was also chronically in debt. In addition this man was treasurer of a university club, heaven knows why. His parents were wealthy people but kept him short on purpose to try to teach him the value of money. Silly

75

idea, really. They had not had much success. Ditchling worked out a particularly mean little scheme and put it into effect. He stole some of the club subscription money, paid part of it, forging his friend's name, to a member of the gaming group to whom he owed it, fiddled the club account book to show for certain where this money had come from and then made certain of visiting the friend when he was making up the accounts. Ditchling then 'discovered' the fraud and theft and calmly proceeded to blackmail his friend. Luckily this chap was so furious at being framed and at the same time so frightened he wouldn't be believed that he told his father the whole story. The father paid the blackmail at once and removed his son from the university and sent him abroad. But he also told the whole story to the Master of the college, who promptly sent Ditchling away, too. The police could not act on the blackmail, though the Master reported it to them, because the father refused to supply any evidence. The son had already destroyed the falsified pages of the account book and made a new correct entry. The money was back in the cash box. The boy's debts were all paid. Nor could they act on the suspicions of one or two tradesmen who had notified small thefts. There was no real evidence. But when a young London free-lance journalist, calling himself Jimmy Dice, was thought to have had something to do with breaking up a home and causing a suicide we were not altogether surprised to find his real name was Jeremy Ditchling. Now d'you see what I mean?'

'How could I fail to?' said Hugh. 'It's a fascinating story and many things are now clear to me that were only vague rumours all through my third year.'

'What did you go to Neots Lane to find?' asked Mitchell, his voice sharpening. 'Or to get?'

Hugh opened his eyes wide, still frantically stalling.

'Oh, Superintendent,' he protested. 'Surely you aren't accusing *me* of practising blackmail? Why, I never saw Jeremy at all after he went down until—'

'Until?'

'I ran across him in the Strand and we had a drink – to chat over old times. He'd written to me occasionally but I hadn't tried to contact him. We met once or twice after that. And then,' Hugh went on, desperately inventing, 'then he said one day wouldn't I run down for dinner and see the bungalow. And I said – I said I'd write, which I did and—'

'That's all right,' said Mitchell. 'You'll do better in court when you've had more practice, I don't doubt. Just now I'm asking you for the truth.'

'And I'm witholding it – just now,' said Hugh firmly, returning to reality without any noticeable jolt.

'Very well, Mr. Mellanby. But there is such a thing as obstructing—'

'I know. At the moment I'm not obstructing anything, I assure you. Jeremy's death was entirely opportune as far as I'm concerned. I'll go so far as to say that. I'll also say that I am practically certain that nothing I could tell you has the slightest bearing on it – on the death, I mean.'

'That's for me to judge,' said Mitchell, stiffly. On this far from cordial note Hugh took his leave.

*　　*　　*

Sir John Drewson arrived back from Switzerland in the early evening. He came alone. Mrs. Wood, his secretary, had stayed behind in Zürich for a few days to get out his personal report on what he had seen, edit his notes and write it all up in her usual efficient manner. She was due in England about the middle of the following week.

Sir John explained all this to Superintendent Mitchell at Scotland Yard, where he had driven direct from London Airport in a taxi, not even taking his luggage to his flat first.

'I felt I had to see you immediately over this horrible business,' he told Mitchell.

The latter nodded. Sir John was a short man, with a

lean elderly, much-lined face that had once been extremely handsome and still held a good deal of charm. He had an air of authority but did not attempt to impose any upon the people he met. This accounted for much of his popularity in ruling circles, where an enthusiasm for social reform is generally regarded cautiously, if not with actual suspicion.

'I'm afraid I haven't any more news for you than you have collected from the papers,' said Mitchell, 'but I think you can help us on one definite point, at least.'

'Anything,' said Sir John. 'Anything at all.'

'Thank you. The main difficulty is to fix the actual time of death. We know that your car was abandoned between nine-thirty and ten in Fulham, so Mr. Ditchling cannot have been put in it after that. We also know from your housekeeper at Drews Cottage that Mr. Ditchling visited you the evening before.'

'He came to see me about—'

'Just a minute, if you don't mind, sir. He left you, according to her, at about seven, or just before. We have no knowledge of his movements after he took the field path from the back of your garden.'

'So you have – let's see – fourteen hours or so, at some point in which he died. Did he die in the car?'

'We can't be sure of that, either. But we ought to be able to narrow the time when he was put in the boot. I take it he was not there when you left your home to go to the airport, nor when you arrived there?'

Sir John shook his head, sadly.

'The suitcases, you mean?' he said. 'My luggage, or rather mine and Mrs. Wood's. You see, we were taking only a small case each, because we expected to be away for only two days. I usually travel by air these days. My suitcase, even the larger one, is always light. We were starting early in the morning. We did not bother to unlock the boot. We simply put the cases on the back seat inside the car.'

Mitchell looked very disappointed. Sir John smiled ruefully. 'Of course he can't have been in the boot at that time,' he said, 'but I haven't got the proof you want. I'm so sorry.'

There was a short silence, then Sir John spoke again.

'I was going to tell you about Ditchling's visit to me,' he said. 'I think it may help you if I do so, and it can't harm the poor fellow now, can it?'

Mitchell shook his head gravely. He did not take Sir John's compassionate view of the deceased but he was curious to know what his relations with him had been.

'As we were near neighbours,' Sir John began, 'we naturally came across one another casually soon after he arrived at the bungalow. In fact my housekeeper, Mrs. Heath, found him wandering in my garden. He had used the footpath from his place and walked through a garden gate I have that opens into it, instead of climbing the stile just round the next bend of the path. An understandable mistake.'

'And a well-known way of striking up an acquaintance,' said the superintendent.

'Yes. It could have been that, I suppose. I know he had a dubious record. I always thought it was weakness rather than a really vicious trend. He was too clever for his moral character: the balance was upset.'

Remembering his visitor's eminence in social science, Mitchell made no comment on this.

'Well, as I said, it was not long before we met near my house. He seemed very lonely and quite incompetent in his domestic arrangements, according to local gossip that came to me through Mrs. Heath. I understood that he had isolated himself in order to write a novel, so I invited him along to dinner one evening. He was, in many ways, interesting to talk to. Not self-conscious about his origins, spoke very nicely and affectionately of his parents—'

'His father nearly threw him out after he was sent down from Oxbridge. But Jimmy took himself off instead. He had the lolly – I mean, the money, tucked away and could afford a few months in London to find his feet again. His father paid up for him at the university. Didn't know about the blackmail until long after Jimmy had spent it. Thought his disgrace was simply on account of the fraud. But perhaps he never told you the full story.'

'Oh dear!' Sir John looked very distressed. 'I seem to have been rather simple over this.'

'He was a professional con man,' answered the superintendent. 'He only stole when he was in a jam or when he saw something he fancied. If he'd stuck to getting money out of generous people he might be alive now, I think.'

'But this is *dreadful*!' Sir John groaned, more upset than before. 'It must explain why he came to see me that evening. It was to do with one of our girls. At Drews Court, you know.'

'I know of the approved school there,' said Mitchell, carefully controlling his sudden interest. 'Go on, sir.'

'I won't tell you her name. At least, not unless you insist. But Ditchling had been meeting her in the woods and – well – he was afraid he'd got her into trouble. He *said* he'd come to tell me he wanted to marry her, but she was under age, and he was afraid her parents wouldn't consent.'

'Good God!' exclaimed the superintendent.

His exclamation derived from the extreme unlikelihood of this proposition ever having entered Jimmy Dice's head. Especially in connection with Mavis Henning, the girl in Miss Pope's charge, the young prostitute and shop-lifter of fourteen, whose fingerprints were all over the bungalow and who was supposed to be undergoing reform at the approved school.

'You doubt his intention?' said Sir John, and sighed heavily. 'In any case he can never carry it out now. And the girl, poor child— I shall have to warn Miss Pope.'

'I shouldn't take any steps yourself, sir,' said Mitchell. 'If Miss Pope suspects there is anything wrong with the girl she'll have a medical consultation and get it sorted

out. They have ways of dealing with that sort of thing –
special homes—'

He left the rest of it vague. It wasn't any business of
the old boy's, though he did look so interested. Anyway, he must know all this already.

'I'm sure you are right,' said Sir John, and got up to
leave. 'That is all I can say. As Mrs. Heath has already
told you, I let him out of the garden gate and saw him
start up the footpath into the woods. Very shortly
afterwards Hugh Mellanby arrived by car. He said he
was expected at the bungalow for dinner, but his host
was not there so he had decided to call on me to learn
if Ditchling had been taken ill or anything. I told him I
had only just taken leave of Ditchling and asked him
in for a drink, to give the boy who had just left time to
get back home. I may have mentioned that he was
upset about a personal matter. No, perhaps I decided
not to. Hugh is a barrister and naturally rather curious
about other people's private affairs. I don't mean in
any nasty way, of course. They get a habit of questioning. I know Hugh well, of course. A friend of my niece,
but you already know all that.'

'Yes.'

'Shall I have to appear at the inquest?'

'I'm afraid so.'

'In that case I will come up again the day after
tomorrow. I must go to Southfield tomorrow morning.
I have a great many things to see to, both there and in
town. You have both addresses, I think. I shall be at
my flat tonight.'

'Very good, sir. May I say that I appreciate your
coming to see me at once. Speed is the essential thing
in all our inquiries.'

'Quite so. Quite so.'

Sergeant Jones escorted Sir John along the corridors
and stairways to the outer world where another taxi
had already been called and loaded with his suitcase,
overcoat, umbrella and briefcase which he had left in
charge of the police porter on the door. He drove to

his flat and promptly summoned Belinda by telephone.

She arrived, feeling very young, rather shaken and when she saw his tired, sad face, very guilty. With a catch in her voice she said, 'I can't tell you how sorry I am—'

'Don't try,' he answered, kindly. 'Come and give me a kiss instead.'

That brought tears, but Sir John fetched drinks and presently they both felt better. Belinda gave her uncle a full, careful, completely truthful account of all she had seen, done and learned of the affair. She also delivered a message from her boss, excusing her attendance the next day if that would help, and a message from Hugh, offering his car, if it would serve, for Belinda to drive her uncle down to Drews Cottage.

'Very kind, very kind,' Sir John said and smiled at her anxious face. 'But I won't put any of you out. I have already hired a car for the job. As I have a full day's work to do down there and have to be back here the day after, I have arranged to leave from here at seven in the morning. I'm afraid that would be much too early for you, wouldn't it?'

Belinda, with a scarlet face, agreed that it might be. Sir John, his arm round her, gave her another kiss, warm and totally forgiving and took her out to dinner.

CHAPTER NINE

SUPERINTENDENT MITCHELL and Sergeant Jones travelled down to Southfield early the next morning, arriving in the little town before nine o'clock. They had purposely not given any warning of their visit at Drews Court in case the girl Mavis should hear of it and run away before they arrived.

They went first to Southfield police station to report their presence and to hear of any local developments. But there was no news for them. The bungalow remained locked; no one had been seen near it. The guard, discreetly posted among the trees bordering its wild, overgrown garden, had nothing to report. The place seemed to be quite deserted. If it did, indeed, belong to the mysterious Mr. Burt, he had certainly not come forward to claim the property, dispose of the furniture or let the place to another tenant. No one had come forward, which was highly suspicious. Since the popular Press had given the story a great deal of importance and had made it a front page, large-picture feature, it seemed odd that the owner of the bungalow showed no interest. But it confirmed the superintendent's guess that Jimmy Dice, or Ditchling, had been up to no good there and, moreover, was working under orders. Mr. Burt's orders. So had he disobeyed them or ignored them? Or failed through no fault of his own? Was his death a penalty for failure, a revenge, or an accident? In police jargon foul play was suspected, but there was still no proof of it.

'Jimmy never actually got across you here for anything, did he?' Mitchell asked the county detective-chief-inspector, a man of the name of Carfax, who was at Southfield to meet him.

'No. Actually we hadn't identified him under that name. We knew him as a writer, likely to be a bit eccentric on that account. When we understood he was running after the Drews Court bunch we weren't surprised and there was nothing we could do, except warn the board of governors of the fact that local lads, plus our author, were playing the tomcat round the place.'

'Exactly. But this must have been more serious. Young Mavis had been visiting the bungalow.'

'So I heard. Actually I've had a word with Miss Pope.'

'When?'

'Day before yesterday. Didn't you want her to know?'

'Did you go up there or get her on the blower?'

'I phoned her.'

'They listen in, you know. Tap wires and that sort of thing. These London kids are up to anything. Perhaps they wouldn't be able to in this case. I wouldn't know. Would you?'

This series of implied criticism annoyed Inspector Carfax. He said, stiffly, 'When do you intend to go up to Drews Court, sir? I have one or two fairly urgent—'

'Don't let me keep you,' Mitchell answered, equably. 'Jones and I will get along at once. I hope it won't be necessary to take this girl into custody. Can't tell at all yet. Depends when she visited the bungalow. By invitation or by "breaking". That sort of thing. I hope she'll talk. She hasn't got a good reputation for co-operating. Been in the juvenile court several times with findings of guilt in each case.'

'I don't know anything about the girls up there. But I take my hat off to Miss Pope. She manages to keep reasonable control of them without promoting riots. I wouldn't care for her job, I can tell you.'

They parted on more friendly terms in complete agreement over the difficulties of Miss Pope's work. Sergeant Jones drove out of the town on the London road and turned off up Neots Lane. Both men left the car near the bungalow, went up to it, tried the doors and looked in through the windows.

They had been there less than three minutes when a man in a mackintosh came up to them.

'It's all right, constable,' the superintendent said, explaining who he was. 'Just having a look round. Owner not turned up yet?'

'No one's been except yourselves, sir,' the man answered, boredom and disgust in his voice.

'Bad luck. It's important all the same.'

'Yes, sir.'

They drove off.

'That chap's on the spot, all right, which was what I wanted to check,' Mitchell said and relapsed into silence.

They passed Sir John Drewson's cottage before turn-

ing towards the big closed gates of Drews Court. While
Jones was opening them Mitchell noticed a pale blue
and grey Vanguard standing near the open doors of a
wooden garage at one side of the cottage. Kept on the
hire-car, he thought, and then remembered that Sir
John was returning to London the next day and could
have only just arrived. He was early at that, Mitchell
thought, but remembered also the man's air of energy
and enthusiasm and decided that he was one of those
who had the start-at-dawn habit.

The two men were admitted to the school by a thin
woman in a severe dark-blue uniform dress, who
explained that she was the second in command to
Miss Pope. She seemed to be upset and became even
more distraught when Mitchell told her who he was.
But she took the visitors to Miss Pope's room and left
them there, saying in an agitated voice that the
principal would come directly.

'Crisis,' said Mitchell, laconically. 'What's the
betting Mavis has scarpered?'

Miss Pope, hurrying into the room a few minutes
later, confirmed this.

'It must have been during the night,' she said, in a
distracted voice. 'None of the other girls will say anything. Two of her friends made excuses for her at
breakfast. Said she had a headache and wasn't coming
down. They do that sort of thing frequently; usually on
purpose to disturb us, interrupt our breakfast and so
on, get a fuss made of them. So we generally play it
down unless it sounds genuine. This quite obviously
wasn't genuine. The girl who told me was half giggling
all the time. Naturally. She had a double joke to enjoy,
from her point of view, since Mavis wasn't there at all.
Matron went up directly after breakfast and found her
bed empty, though the bedclothes were rumpled.'

'When was this?' Mitchell asked.

'About two hours ago. We've searched the whole
house thoroughly and they're still going over the
grounds.'

'But you haven't reported it yet?'

'Oh yes, I have. I rang them at Southfield just now. About a quarter of an hour ago. When I had made sure she wasn't hiding in the house. I was just going to ring Sir John Drewson when you arrived.'

Mitchell was puzzled and then remembered.

'As chairman of the governors?'

'Yes. He is always so good to us. So helpful and understanding. He was due back at the cottage this morning, Mrs. Heath told me yesterday.'

The telephone on Miss Pope's desk began to ring. She listened, said, 'He's here now,' and held out the receiver to the superintendent.

'Mitchell here— So I've heard from Miss Pope— She'll be on her way to London if she hasn't already got there. What?— Yes, certainly. But I think I know where she'll turn up.'

He put back the receiver, then took it up again to get Scotland Yard. After giving his news there, followed by some instructions, he ended his call and turned back to Miss Pope.

'It's unfortunate,' he said. 'Also a bit puzzling. I suppose you have newspapers about the place?'

'Oh, yes. We're a school, not a prison. We try to get the girls to take a reasonable interest in the world at large. Their main difficulty is their narrow little minds focused entirely on themselves.'

'So Mavis will have heard about Ditchling's death and so on?'

'It's been one of the biggest thrills since I came here. That sounds horribly callous, but they like to exaggerate everything. The more melodrama the better. They all knew him by sight, but most of them disliked him. In their own limited field they are pretty knowledgeable and shrewd. As far as Mavis was concerned I was very worried. I was sure she was meeting him. She's a thorough liar. It's impossible to take anything she says at its face value, even when she looks completely reasonable and innocent.'

Mitchell nodded. The girl's record was already a formidable one for her age.

'How did she react to Ditchling's death?' he asked.

'That worried me more than anything,' Miss Pope answered. 'She didn't even seem surprised. I was afraid it was shock. I had a talk with her about it and she simply said, "Why pick on me? It was Beryl he was after."'

'Was he?'

'No. I don't think so. Beryl was never seen with him. She cried a good deal when she heard of his death, but she's a very unstable emotional girl. She cries at the least thing.'

'D'you think Mavis has got herself into real trouble with Ditchling? She isn't pregnant, is she?'

'No,' said Miss Pope, firmly. 'I'm sure she isn't. We take great care to check for that, of course.'

Mitchell nodded. He did not repeat to Miss Pope what Sir John had told him. It was a typical lie on Jimmy's part.

Clearly there was nothing more to be done at Drews Court, Mitchell decided. He went back into Southfield for a short conference with Carfax. A close search of the woods near Drews Court had already begun. Inquiries were being made at houses in the neighbourhood, at the railway station and at garages, filling stations and roadside cafés in the county, where lorries might have pulled in during the night.

Mitchell did not discourage any of this. It was correct routine stuff and not in his jurisdiction. But he did not expect it to produce results. He drove back to London feeling fairly confident that Mavis would turn up in a day or two where she always did when she ran away. Not at the home of her parents where she had never got anything but blows and harsh words, but at her old grandmother's house in Bermondsey, where all her lies and fantasies about herself received a futile, doting welcome.

But this time the superintendent was wrong. After

two days Mavis was found. Her body was seen, submerged, entangled in weeds, by some young Southfield
boys who were trying to fish from the bridge over the
river on the London road. One of them had dropped
his line into the water and had crept down the steep
bank with a long stick to try to retrieve it. While he was
poking through the reeds he had seen a large bundle
just underneath the water. He had pushed his stick
into it and an arm showed itself. He rushed back to his
friends who all crowded down the bank to see. Then
they trooped back to Southfield and told the first
constable they met what they had found.

The news was relayed immediately to Scotland Yard
and to Drews Court. Miss Pope, shocked and distressed
and for the first time in her sensible dedicated life
feeling unequal to the occasion, telephoned to Sir
John's house. She was answered by Mrs. Heath. Sir
John, as she might have remembered, was in London
again and likely to remain there for the rest of the week.
By the time she had finished the call her panic was
subsiding. She called her staff together to discuss with
them the best way to give the tragic news to the school.
Later in the day she wrote to Sir John, though she knew
he would have already learned from the newspapers
and perhaps from the police what had happened.

Meanwhile the search continued in the woods and
fields round Drews Court for anything that might help
to show why and when Mavis Henning had met her
death. At the same time a forensic pathologist arrived
at Southfield public mortuary to examine the body.
Superintendent Mitchell had managed to secure Dr.
Wing for the job, since this case was almost certainly
linked in some way with that of Jeremy Ditchling.

The pathologist's findings confirmed this view. The
girl's body showed no signs whatever of violence. She
had drowned, fully clothed in jeans, a sweater and a
mock-suède jacket. She had died quietly, without a
struggle of any kind, it seemed. Remembering Ditchling's death and the girl's association with him, Dr.

Wing took specimens for analysis. The result of this was exactly what he suspected. Mavis had taken a heavy dose of barbiturate before she drowned.

'She must have got it from Ditchling,' Mitchell said. 'Or from the same source as he got his own supply. This looks like suicide, following Ditchling's death. Dr. Wing says she'd been dead about two days when she was found in the river. No signs of pregnancy.'

The superintendent was at Southfield again in response to a special call from Inspector Carfax.

'That means she was already dead when they found out at Drews Court she was missing,' the inspector said. 'I've been into it pretty thoroughly with Miss Pope and the girls in the same dormitory as Mavis. They're scared just now and I think they spoke the truth. Apparently Mavis climbed out of the window and slid down a water-pipe as she had done a good many times before when she wanted a night out. Usually she was away only a couple of hours. The other girls used to listen for her and lower a rope one of them kept under a loose board in the floor. This helped her to climb up again.'

'Did Miss Pope never suspect?'

'Of course she did. But the girls were too smart for her. Drews Court is a school, not a prison. Miss Pope is excellent for the easier sort of girl, who can be put back on the rails and feel happier that way. Personally I think Mavis ought never to have been sent there. She was a bad influence on the others. Ought to have been at a borstal and a secure one at that. One or two of the wrong sort at an approved school makes havoc.'

'You're right there. And it's worse with boys. Mavis must have thought a lot of Jimmy to ditch herself at fourteen, poor kid.'

'It's not in character,' insisted Inspector Carfax. 'I never saw a harder face on a pro than on that little black-eyed bitch. Figure of a girl of twenty. Hard and sly, too. She'd pretty well ditched her life already, but I'd swear she wasn't the suicide type.'

Mitchell did not argue the point. He had never seen Mavis alive and only knew her from her record. Instead he asked, 'Have any of those girls an idea where she was off to? Did she say she wasn't coming back? Did she borrow money? Did she take anything with her, handbag, for instance?'

'I asked all that,' the inspector said. 'Nothing.'

Mitchell nodded approval of the inspector's thoroughness. He felt he had come up against a blank wall. London had nothing to offer. Mavis had not been seen in any of her usual hideouts or with any of her known friends. It was doubtful if she had gone even as far as Southfield. Certainly she had not used public transport in the town. Most of it had stopped before she left Drews Court. She would have been noticed among the few bus passengers going home late. The railway station was equally unhelpful. Again, through traffic on the London road was a possibility. For this reason Scotland Yard had issued a photograph of the dead girl to the newspapers.

The superintendent, casting about for something to do before he left the little town to go back to London, suggested that Carfax and he might take another walk along the path through the woods, more to encourage the searchers there than in any hope of turning up a clue themselves.

But as they got out of the police car near the bridge over the river, meaning to enter the woods from the towpath at the point where the footpath joined it, they met two of Carfax's men, moving towards them with every sign of excitement.

'Just come across these, sir,' one of them said, holding up a polythene bag. 'Together in a trodden down area of undergrowth ten yards from the path. Traced some footprints leading to the area, but they're very blurred. More than two lots.'

Evidently the man had rehearsed his report which he gave fluently in formal jargon.

Inspector Carfax took the bag, peered through the

polythene at the contents and handed it to Mitchell. The latter glanced at it, handed it back and said, 'Good work. We'd better take it in and have a look at it.'

The find consisted of a girl's scarf in mohair wool knitted in stripes of yellow and pink, and a button mould without a front to it. The latter caused both men to exclaim.

'D'you know what I think?' Mitchell said. 'The missing button off Ditchling's jacket.'

'Could be.'

'It's the same size and colour. More than that, though. Take another look.'

Carfax did so, but got no further.

'Unless I'm very much mistaken,' Mitchell said, 'this was not only a button. It was a camera, transistor type. I can't prove it. The works have gone. The experts may be able to give an opinion.'

'If it is, that means?'

'No idea, except that if it really is the missing button Ditchling's suspected blackmailing efforts had a firm basis.'

'What about the scarf?'

'That should be easy. Send it up to Drews Court with one of your chaps. The girls ought to know if it belonged to Mavis Henning.'

The dead girl's photograph duly appeared in the daily Press, which was glad to have it as the parents had none and the grandmother only a tinted affair made when the child was two.

Hugh saw it at breakfast on the day it appeared. Before that he had taken very little interest in the drowning, except that it involved Southfield in another mystery and made him wonder what further mischief Jeremy had been up to in the district. He had discussed the matter briefly with Belinda but as she had not seen her uncle since the night of his return she had no news to give Hugh from that source.

The appearance of the photograph was a shock. It

broke through his careful aloofness, his secrecy, his guarded attitude to the police. He saw that now he had to act and act quickly. In his sudden confusion and discomfiture he acknowledged for the first time his own inexperience. He could not afford to go wrong at this point. Too much was at stake.

As soon as possible he tried to get in touch with Mitchell. He heard that the Superintendent himself was away and would not be available, but his next in command would see him.

In considerable agitation he went early to his chambers. No one else had arrived. Barrett, the clerk, was surprised to see him.

'Don't tell me the great man is in court today?' Hugh asked, fearfully, feeling even more incompetent for not being aware of Warrington-Reeve's time-table.

'On the contrary,' said a voice behind him. 'What's he want, Barrett?'

Warrington-Reeve swept towards his own room. He never moved slowly and Hugh started off at once in pursuit, afraid he would be shut out and have to knock at a closed door.

'I'd like to ask your advice, sir,' he stammered. 'It's a – rather private – concerns a friend—'

'Stop blathering in public, then,' said Reeve, turning in the doorway. 'Come in, come in, and shut the door behind you.'

When they were both inside Warrington-Reeve sat down and motioned Hugh to do the same. But the young man instead pulled an envelope from his pocket and took from it the photograph he had found at the bungalow, together with the photograph and paragraph he had cut from that morning's newspaper. He held them out to his chief.

'It's the same girl, you see, sir,' he said. 'That photograph was being used to blackmail a friend of mine. But I don't think it's him. He swears it isn't. Where do you think I ought to go from here, sir?'

'To Scotland Yard for a start,' said Warrington-

Reeve. 'But before that you can tell me the whole story, if you like.'

'I would have gone to the Yard this morning, but Superintendent Mitchell – that's the one in charge of the case, isn't there. They said he'd be away most probably till tomorrow. I refused to speak to anyone else.'

'I see. Well, come on, give me the story. I can't advise you until I've heard it, can I?'

CHAPTER TEN

SUPERINTENDENT MITCHELL, who disapproved openly and often of coming to any sort of conclusion without evidence, secretly decided that Ditchling and young Mavis had both been killed with the same purpose in view, to prevent their threatened exposure of Mr. Burt. What was more likely? The man had kept his identity hidden with much more than ordinary skill and success. When he had put a foot wrong was first in employing the young man at all, and secondly, much more dangerous, trying to quarantine him by sending him down to the bungalow.

The first mistake was probably inevitable. Expanding his range to blackmail as a sideline of his usual well-planned robberies, Mr. Burt had clearly been afraid to show himself to his victims. Jimmy must conduct the actual negotiations, even perhaps provide the evidence, the photo, the tape, the eye-witness. Jimmy was an educated type, Burt would think. You could trust him to play fair if you paid him well for it. That was what he would think – at first.

But things must have gone wrong. Had Jimmy refused to pay up, after collecting the lolly? There was nothing Burt could do about that except some strong-arm stuff which would put Jimmy out of his service for good, if not out of this world. Or had Jimmy got a line on Burt himself? Had he discovered in his quick, devious, cold-blooded, sly way who Burt really was? Had he begun to blackmail the boss?

'Was that why Burt lent him the bungalow, sir?' Sergeant Jones asked. 'To keep him out of London while he changed his own address and so on?'

'No. It isn't any good our speculating,' said Mitchell, severely, annoyed with himself for airing his own guesses. 'It could have been in order to plan his murder. But I've nothing to support that, yet,' he added, quickly. 'I'm just keeping him top of the list for the double murder. I've got Frank working on that angle now.'

'*Working* on it?'

'Well, yes. If Jimmy found out who Burt is, we have to ask what is he likely to have found? The first thing would be did he know about Burt's main line of business. We know Jimmy knew Len, so the answer there is yes. What could Jimmy have picked up by knowing a list of Burt's operations? That's what I hope Frank will work out for me.'

'How?'

'Take all the raids of the same nature as the one that failed in Wandsworth. See if there is any possible common factor – location – personnel – results – type of goods stolen, money included. Then – possible disposal – possible source of knowledge of goods and delivery – mode of delivery – firm's car, hire-car, taxi, security vehicle etc. Violence used – weapons, if any. Insurance of goods and/or personnel. Routine stuff, I know,' he said, seeing a look of boredom creep over Jones's young keen face, 'but the way to crack open most of our problems.'

'Yes, sir.'

Having smothered his speculations in a heavy layer of method, Mitchell turned to a report that had just come in from Ireland.

'Leaving all that to Frank,' he said, 'we're going over

to Dublin to have a chat with Len. They've located him and they'll pull him in if necessary.'

'Can they do that?'

'Not really. They've nothing on him there and nor have we really, here, except taking away and driving that Humber without the owner's consent. We found it the same day, remember. It doesn't count a larceny, only a misdemeanour.'

'Isn't that a charge, all the same?'

'If he says anything useful it might be held over till he comes back to this country. Not worth getting him extradited. The fine wouldn't cover it.'

'When do we go, sir? Will we be stopping the night?'

'I hope not. We leave here in half an hour from now.'

They found Len Smithson waiting for them at the headquarters of the Dublin police. He had been picked up that morning as he was going to work.

'Made no kind of fuss over it at all,' Mitchell was told. 'Came along like a lamb. We've nothing on him so far this time and he knows it. Says he's not scared of extradition because you've nothing on him, either.'

'He's a bit optimistic there,' answered Mitchell.

Len greeted him calmly but warily as a long-unseen but potentially dangerous acquaintance. Mitchell came to the point straight away.

'You took a Humber from Chelsea and left it less than an hour later just off Garratt Lane. Before that you took Sir John Drewson's Jaguar from London Airport. Where did you pick up Jimmy Dice's body and what were you going to do with it?'

'*Me pick up*— You must be bats, super. It took me all me time, in that traffic—'

He stopped, realizing how much he had implied, in his shock and sudden terror. Then, deciding he couldn't have held out on that, anyway, he stared at Mitchell, waiting for the next, inevitable question. It came, briefly.

'What time did you take Sir John's car?'

95

'Must have been all of nine.'

'You left the Jaguar at a quarter to ten.'

'Who told you that?'

Len's surprise was genuine and Mitchell smiled.

'Houses have windows, you know. And people who look out through them.'

This really startled Len. It was something that had not occurred to him at all. He realized that Mitchell was still talking.

'—so, as Sir John left the car at eight o'clock we have only your word for it that you did not use the next hour and a half dealing with Dice's body. What were you doing before you arrived at the airport? Had you arranged beforehand to take the Jag? Did Jimmy tell you Sir John was going abroad?'

Len's horror and astonishment grew to breaking proportions. He saw now exactly where his choice of the Jag was leading him. He had never worked this out before. It had certainly been conversation about air travel that had led up to the idea about the airport. And from that to Sir John's Jaguar. Also the fact that he had quite a good selection of Jaguar keys on his ring.

'I wasn't doing nothing except eat me breakfast,' he said, sullenly. 'Who's this character, Dice, you keep mentioning? No one I know. Got hisself croaked, did he? I seen nothing in the papers about no Dice.'

He gave a short laugh, recognizing a half-joke in what he had said. Mitchell was not amused.

'You knew him all right. As Dice, I suspect, certainly as Ditchling. That was why, when you saw his photograph, you crossed over to Belfast the same afternoon. You shouldn't run home to mother every time, Len. She does her best, but it helps us more than you.'

Len's face darkened.

'Leave her out of it,' he said. 'You think you can pin taking and driving away on me. The Jag, I admit.'

'That Humber, too,' said Mitchell.

'I deny it. Anyway, you found the Jag within forty-eight hours, didn't you? So what?'

Mitchell looked at him. Len must know as well as he did that he would not have come over to Ireland on a minor charge, even if it could be proved against him. There was more behind his visit. Now was the moment to bring it up.

'So I think you can help my inquiries,' Mitchell said. 'Any help you can give may be taken into consideration in making charges against you.'

'I don't know nothing,' said Len, stoutly, but already he was reckoning up the possible cost of breaking altogether with Mr. Burt.

'If you'll answer a few questions I might be able to judge of that,' Mitchell said. He saw the man was wavering. He knew he must play him very carefully.

Len made no answer, but neither did he attempt to go. He lit another of his interminable cigarettes and sat smoking it in rapid nervous pulls, staring at the floor.

'Do you know who this man Burt really is?' Mitchell asked. 'Cover trade – or job?'

'No.'

'Have you ever been to his flat in Kilburn?'

Len looked up, startled. So they did know something. How much? Was it any good holding out?

'What if I have?'

'Does he live there? Is the woman who calls herself Florrie Dean his wife?'

Len's derisive laugh answered that one.

'I thought not. Is he married?'

'Ask me another.'

'Does he live off Dean's earnings?'

'Look, mister,' Len said, bitterly. 'Burt doesn't confide in me personally. Nor in anyone. He's one of the bosses. He can pick and choose— Seems like he's fallen down on that, just lately. But it's no bloody good asking me for his private life. I can have ideas, but so can you.'

'I certainly can,' said Mitchell, beginning to lose patience. 'Just now my idea is you're not going to be much use to me and I'd better get on with making a charge and seeing you get brought back to answer it.'

'Go ahead,' said Len. 'You can't prove nothing but taking and driving away.'

'I can hold you on suspicion of being concerned in the murder of Jeremy Ditchling, alias Jimmy Dice and of Mavis Henning.'

Len stumbled to his feet, looking wildly about him. He saw a ring of interested faces, uniformed figures. He sat down again.

'You've got nothing on me,' he muttered, but it was clear he had lost his defiance.

'Where did you meet Ditchling?' Mitchell demanded.

'Pub in Notting Hill. Blue Boar.'

'When?'

'Couple of months back.'

'Why?'

'Burt said meet 'im there. It was where he fetched us from to go to his flat. Miss Dean's flat.'

'Yes. Go on.'

'Ditchling – Dice – Jimmy, he was with him. They'd fixed something between them. Nothing to do with me. Wanted me to drive this bloke, Ditchling, to an address.'

'Drive? Had you got a car of your own?'

'Not likely.' Len looked more surly than ever. 'I was working for a car-hire firm. On my way back from a job. There was time to fit Burt's chap in. I took him along and dropped him where the boss said and took my car back to the depot.'

Mitchell wondered how often Len had earned a bit on the side at his employer's expense. Well, if they didn't ever check on his petrol or mileage it was their own lookout. He nodded at Len. It was what he expected. A minor part in one of Burt's schemes, no questions asked, good pay, probably.

'Where did you drop Ditchling? What was the address he was going to?'

'Think they'd give me that? I told you, I put him off, where he said. He walked back up the street. Wasn't likely to stop at a house while I could see where he went. Not him.'

'What district was it in?'

'Bermondsey.'

This answer took Mitchell by surprise. He had expected somewhere in the West End or one of the wealthy residential areas. Bermondsey did not seem to offer bright prospects for blackmail. But he thought of factories and offices and managing directors and decided to keep an open mind.

'That pub, the Blue Boar,' he said. 'Is it a regular meeting place for your lot?'

'Has been up to now,' said Len, reluctantly. 'But he'll have the sense to give it up, if he hasn't done so already, or I don't know Burt.'

'You didn't like Jimmy, did you?'

'That's my business.'

'It's mine if you disliked him so much you killed him.'

Len's face whitened, but he said nothing.

'What did he do to you? Blackmail – or protection?'

There was no answer.

'Very well,' said Mitchell. 'I'm going back tonight. You'd be well advised not to try any tricks, Len. We may want you again. I assure you we shan't lose track of you. Don't complicate things by getting into trouble here, will you?'

'Have I ever?' said Len, indignantly.

'He hasn't and that's a fact,' said the Irish superintendent, with a grin. 'Perhaps the climate over here suits him better, eh, Len?'

But Len found it impossible to share a joke with a rozzer. He merely scowled. Besides, these questions had been too near the mark. They made him feel quite ill in his inside.

On getting back to London Mitchell found two things to interest him; an urgent request from Hugh for an interview and a word from Inspector Hall, asking to report progress. Mitchell decided to see the latter straightaway. The young barrister could wait till the morning. He had enough on his plate for that day and he did not expect much help from that quarter. On the other hand Hall had made slight, but significant progress.

'Go ahead, Frank,' Mitchell told him, as the inspector went into his room.

'It's like this,' Hall began. 'I started on your suggestion at the insurance end, grouping wages and bank raids. Which come to pretty much the same thing, in their relation to the insurers. This didn't give anything to begin with. But when I dug a bit deeper I found that three claims were handled by subsidiaries of the same big firm.'

'How did that work out?'

'Very nicely. The insurance assessors had already begun to wonder. You see, this firm had been stung by two independent claims quite recently, making five in all over the last year.'

'So you think Burt works in one of these concerns, gets his ideas from the clients and goes on from there?'

'Something of that sort. My guess would be he's in the main firm rather than the subsidiaries, as the jobs cover the lot and have all been done in London.'

'Right. You can now find evidence to support your guess. Have you made any moves yet?'

'I've an appointment with the managing director this afternoon. I wanted to see you first.'

'Sure the managing director isn't the chap we want?'

'I saw the chairman of the directors yesterday, sir. Actually they've been worried themselves over this series of big claims, as I said. They've got their solicitors on to it in a quiet way. Managing director's idea.'

'H'm. Well, you must beat them to it. Go ahead, though I don't see quite how, without making it obvious to a great many people in the business. You've got to find out if there was one single character, from an office boy up to the chairman of the concern, who **knew** enough detail of individual insurance to tip off

our Mr. Burt, if he wasn't Burt himself. Or else someone who could have got access to papers giving the
information.'

'It's bound to start up a lot of gossip, isn't it? I
mean, won't it scare off the bloke we want?'

'He's probably scared enough already with these
murders under investigation. He won't have left the
firm; too obvious. But he'll lay off the money raids, for
a bit, anyway. If you get too close, you may flush him
and he'll try to run. All the better for us.'

Inspector Hall went off to continue his tedious,
complicated and delicate inquiries. Later in the day
Mitchell with Sergeant Jones paid a visit to the Blue
Boar. O'Hara and Corri, who went there for a drink
most evenings in the hope that Mr. Burt would need
their services, were playing darts together when the
two detectives walked in. O'Hara was the first to notice
the newcomers. Though their faces were unfamiliar,
as they did not belong to the local division, he recognized them for what they were.

'Keep playing,' he whispered to Corri, 'and keep your
back to the bar. There's a couple of cops just come in,
but I don't know them so they don't know us.'

' 'Ow you know they'se cops?' Corri growled,
beginning to feel panic.

'Shut your trap! They'll hear you. I know because I
know, see. We got to leave, but quiet. Finish the game.
Go on, your throw.'

Corri threw, but badly, hitting the outer edge of the
board. The general noise in the pub covered the sharp
sound of impact, but Sergeant Jones had happened to
look at the board while Mitchell was securing their
drinks and he saw that this was a strange lapse from the
previous standard of play. He turned back, but he had
made a mental note of the player.

O'Hara brought the game to a close, both men
finished their drinks and then moved quietly to the
door. Jones saw them go.

'They rumbled us,' he said to Mitchell.

'Think so?'

Jones explained his views on the darts episode. Shortly after this the pub began to empty. O'Hara's exit with Corri seemed to have a withering effect on the clientele. They drifted off singly or in small groups and no one else came in. Only a few old men, smoking pipes at a corner table and one or two middle-aged couples, were left. Mitchell went up to the now deserted bar. The landlord had disappeared also; only the barmaid was serving.

'Not very full tonight, are you?' Mitchell said.

'Whose fault is that?'

He smiled at her.

'You tell me.'

'You don't need telling.'

'Bad consciences around here?'

For answer she slapped their mugs of beer on the counter, spilling some of their contents. Mitchell paid her with a note and when she came back from the till with the change she saw a photograph lying under her eyes which made her gasp.

'You recognize him, don't you?' Mitchell said.

'It's that bloke in the papers. I've seen his photo there, haven't I?'

'But he used to come here sometimes?'

'If you know, why do you ask?'

'Look,' said Mitchell. 'You weren't a friend of his, were you?'

'What's it got to do with you?'

'A good deal. Is there any reason why you shouldn't answer a straight question?'

'I don't like questions, mister, straight or crooked. I'm not supposed to gossip about the customers.'

Mitchell told her who he was.

'As if I didn't know!'

'Did Ditchling come here?'

'Sometimes.'

'Who with?'

As there was no answer Mitchell added, 'You don't

want to shield a murderer, do you? Accessory after—'

That moved her.

'How can I remember? He wasn't in all that often. Had different ones with him. Those two that was playing darts, for a start. They come a lot.'

'Yes. Who else?'

'Short square bloke. Spectacles. When he come he always ordered a whisky or a brandy and drank it off quick at the bar. Not speaking.'

'When Ditchling was with him?'

'He wasn't with him. Met him here.'

'I see. And then?'

'They'd leave. Soon as they'd met up, they'd leave.'

'You noticed that because it was unusual?'

'Well, it was, wasn't it? I mean to say—'

'Anyone else met them here?'

'Them other two. And latterly the clergyman. Only seen him the once.'

'*Clergyman!*'

Mitchell could not help his exclamation. The barmaid looked at him with scorn.

'What's so funny about that? Anyone can turn his collar back to front, can't he?'

CHAPTER ELEVEN

HUGH went to Scotland Yard the next morning, much fortified by the presence of Warrington-Reeve, who insisted upon going with him.

'There's a possible case here of obstructing the police,' he said. 'I shall attend as your legal adviser.'

'It's very good of you, sir,' Hugh said, overwhelmed by this offer.

'Self-interest,' snapped Reeve. 'Don't want people in my chambers advertising their ignorance or defiance of the law, whichever it was on your part in this case.'

'A bit of both, I'm afraid,' said Hugh, humbly.

'Teach you a lesson,' Reeve told him.

Superintendent Mitchell was surprised to find eminent counsel in attendance on his young friend. He knew Warrington-Reeve as a highly successful advocate who had at the beginning of his career before the war been employed chiefly on the side of various criminals, usually with startling success. Of late years, with one notable and recent exception, he had, however, usually acted for the Crown, with equal brilliance and from the police point of view, success. Mitchell greeted him with respect and guarded deference. They all sat down and there were a few seconds of complete silence.

'You asked to see me,' Mitchell said, seeing that no one else was going to open the interview. 'What about?'

'This.'

Hugh laid before him the envelope holding the photograph. Mitchell looked at the envelope, noting the '£500' written on it and then drew out the photograph. His face hardened.

'Where did you get this?'

'From the desk in the bungalow.'

'You recognized these people in the photograph?'

'Not at the time, no. Yesterday morning I saw a photograph of the girl in the newspaper.'

'And the man?'

'As you see he's in shadow, with his back to the camera. I don't recognize him.'

'It isn't you?'

'Good God, no!'

Warrington-Reeve interrupted.

'If I may make a suggestion, superintendent. Perhaps Mr. Mellanby had better tell you his story. As he has already told it to me.'

Mitchell looked at the barrister and nodded. Young Mellanby had told his story once. He'd tell it again or just as much of it as his counsel had arranged. Anyway, it wouldn't differ from anything Warrington-Reeve had heard, though it might not be the whole.

'I went to the bungalow in the first place,' Hugh began, 'to buy this photo for a friend of mine who was being blackmailed by Jeremy Ditchling.'

'Who is this friend of yours?'

'Must I give you his name? He asked for my help in the greatest secrecy. He simply didn't dare to go to you people about the blackmail.'

'Why not?'

'He was afraid it would wreck his career. It doesn't matter how much the courts try to hide identity. Mr. A wouldn't help him. His profession is too obvious.'

'I shall have to know who he is.'

'Can I tell you the rest of the story first?'

He glanced at Warrington-Reeve, who nodded.

'This friend of mine had been in my year at Oxbridge, though not in the same college. He also knew Ditchling slightly. He works in a rather poor part of London and comes across all kinds of people.'

'He is a clergyman,' said Mitchell, the light breaking suddenly, 'and he lives and works in Bermondsey.'

Warrington-Reeve smiled. Hugh gasped.

'Never mind how I know,' Mitchell said, making the most of his moral advantage. 'Just go on. Only you needn't try to conceal this man's identity any longer.'

'The girl asked for his help,' Hugh went on. 'Apparently she lived in his parish before she was sent to Drews Court approved school. I don't know if she met Jeremy before or after he went to live at the bungalow, but the blackmail must have been arranged between them. Before, I should think.'

Mitchell did not enlighten him. It was a point he had not checked himself, yet.

'My friend was simple and trusting enough to see this girl alone at the vicarage in the vicar's study. He is only a curate himself. The vicar is an enlightened and hard-working man. He wants to encourage these interviews, really a sort of confession I suppose it is—'

'They work it better in the Roman church,' said Warrington-Reeve. 'The psychology is traditional; it is a ritual, not a personal matter. You do it in church and you don't see the priest. Safer for both parties.'

'Anyway, the girl came about three times,' Hugh said. 'Nothing whatever took place to suggest the situation in the photo.'

'Who let her into the house? Wasn't there a house-keeper or maid or vicar's wife or secretary?'

'On two occasions there was the vicar's wife, who showed her in and let her out again. The last time the vicar's wife let her in and then went out with her husband. The girl must have known this would happen sooner or later.'

'Quite. But what about the photographer?'

Hugh's voice rose in anger.

'That's the damnable part of it. Bob – my friend – suspected nothing until Jeremy called, showed him the photo and asked for five hundred pounds. Bob was appalled, naturally. He said the figure in the picture wasn't him, couldn't possibly be him. Jeremy told him the girl was ready to swear it was. They had been alone in the house. Bob couldn't prove that no one else had called, that there had been no one to take the photograph. With that picture and the girl's evidence – her perjury, rather – it would be easy enough to expose a scandal. Say the girl had got her boy-friend to come in because she was afraid of Bob, and he'd hidden in the vicar's room and taken the photo. Even if they were convicted of blackmail the scandal would stick. It would mean Bob's career in the church would be ruined. It's a real vocation. That's the damnable part of it. It made him believe they could do just what they threatened.'

Hugh stopped, out of breath and overcome by his feelings. Mitchell, inclined now to believe his story, gave him time to recover. Then he said, 'Now tell me what you did when your friend told you the story?'

'Got in touch with Jeremy, of course. It was true what I told you about running into him in the Strand. That was a few months before this thing broke. I knew roughly where I should find him. It was where he asked me to meet him and have a drink and talk over old times. I wasn't keen but I thought he looked ill and depressed, so I agreed.'

'He probably needed a fix or he wouldn't have been so anxious to talk to a friend,' said Mitchell.

'Yes. He drugged, didn't he? Well, I went to this pub—'

'The Blue Boar, Notting Hill,' said Mitchell. 'Where your curate friend went later to try to alter Ditchling's mind over the blackmail.'

'Who told you that?'

'No one. Just putting two and two together.'

'You've got a damned sight more than four in your hand already,' Hugh said, unable to smother his admiration.

'Go on.'

'That's all, really. I had another go at Jeremy, but the dirty beggar wouldn't pull out. I agreed to go down to the bungalow and buy the photo. I went back to Bob to report. He was pretty nearly suicidal that evening. Those two crooks!'

'Two?'

'Oh yes, there was another one with Jeremy. Short fat type, very quiet. There as a witness or bodyguard, do you think?'

'Possibly,' said Mitchell, identifying the unknown as Burt.

'I got Bob to think up a scheme for realizing £500 and said I'd bring the photo back or call their bluff. The idea was that he'd invited me to dinner, Jeremy, I mean, so I was to write accepting the invitation.'

Mitchell nodded.

'I've never been so surprised in my life,' finished Hugh, 'to find him out, the doors unlocked and the photo just lying there inside the desk.'

Again there was silence in the room. Then Mitchell said, 'Your story is very plausible, Mr. Mellanby. There is just one point I don't understand. Why are you still in possession of this photograph, nearly a fortnight after you tell me you took it from the bungalow?'

Hugh was silent. Warrington-Reeve said, 'I told you so'.

With an effort Hugh said, 'At first because Bob was away from London, for a weekend with his people. I tried to ring him up on Monday but he wasn't back because he'd had a touch of 'flu, the vicar said. I wasn't surprised. This business had got him down and he looked ghastly the last time I saw him, just before he left. You can check all this, can't you?'

'Of course,' Mitchell told him. 'But after he was back, did you do nothing about the photo, then?'

'No.'

'Why not? Why not give it to your friend, since he had bought it? Why didn't you produce it when we first got in touch with you?'

Again Hugh fell silent. Again Warrington-Reeve prompted him. 'You'll have to tell him.'

'Yes.' Turning to the superintendent Hugh went on. 'When I got the news of Jeremy's death I felt awful. You see that photo was pretty damning. I know it doesn't show Bob's face, so you could argue it wasn't him. But he'd seen it and he told me he recognized the girl and that she'd had interviews with him. He swore it wasn't him, but he was in a terrible state over the blackmail and after the body was found I began to wonder.'

'You began to wonder if your friend was the murderer?'

Hugh nodded.

'So in order to protect him you suppressed this photograph and your story, which would have led us straight to Mavis Henning and possibly might have saved her life.'

Hugh gulped and hung his head. Warrington-Reeve intervened. 'That does not by any means follow,' he said. 'Mr. Mellanby could not know that there was any urgency about declaring the photograph. He found it in Ditchling's house, but that does not prove it belonged to Ditchling or was taken by Ditchling. It might well have been one of his associates.'

Having made these not very convincing remarks with the maximum of persuasive authority, Warrington-Reeve stood up. Hugh, with some hesitation, followed suit. But Mitchell had not yet finished with him.

'I should like a signed statement of what you've just told me,' he said. 'I must ask you to wait while it is written out.'

'He can write it himself – or dictate it—' Warrington-Reeve said. 'You can't expect literate witnesses to sign the usual jargon. I've already taken notes of what he told me yesterday. What he has just said is precisely the same.'

Warrington-Reeve then left the Yard to return to his chambers, leaving Hugh, feeling thoroughly deflated, to make and sign his statement.

In the course of this proceeding, Mitchell said, 'I've always thought it odd you found the bungalow doors unlocked. With this photograph in the bureau I can't believe that any longer. Ditchling, knowing you were coming for it, would hardly leave it ready to your hand. Even if something happened to send him unexpectedly and urgently away from Southfield. He visited Sir John first, so it could not have been something that would put everything else out of his mind.'

'No.'

'How did you really get in?'

'The small window of the heads. Round the back.'

'And you left the doors unlocked on purpose when you went along to Drews Cottage to see if Ditchling was there?'

'The front door, yes. I went out that way.'

'And after you returned there did you leave it unlocked still?

'Yes. As a kind of message – of defiance. I'd got the photo, you see.'

With this amendment Hugh completed and signed his statement. He then went back to the chambers himself, expecting to be told that his presence there was now superfluous. He was surprised to find a brief on his table and directions from Bassett.

'Mr. Reeve said there is a point on the first page he'd be obliged if you would verify, Mr. Mellanby. He has marked it. He would like a note from you by late afternoon and a further note, where you will find it marked also, by tomorrow morning.'

Relieved and grateful, Hugh thanked the clerk and prepared to settle to his task.

'There was another message Mr. Reeve asked me to convey, sir,' said Barrett. 'If you'll pardon me, I'll repeat his exact words. "Tell the young blighter –" not my expression, Mr. Mellanby, Mr. Reeve's – "that I intend to prevent him getting into further mischief if I have to keep his nose to the grindstone from this time until the case is finished." He said you would know what he meant, sir.'

'Thank you, Barrett,' Hugh answered. 'I know exactly what he meant.'

Before getting to work he rang up Belinda. She answered him briefly. He seldom broke her rule of not being rung up at the office. He apologized now for doing so and asked her if he could come to the flat that evening.

'I'm free when I leave here,' she said, preferring to meet him earlier for a meal.

'I'm up to the eyes. Shall have to work late. Old W-R is on the warpath. I don't want food—'

'But I do.'

'Darling, if you're tough with me I shall cry. I've just been worked over at Scotland Yard.'

'Oh well, come as early as you can.'

'Of course I will. Bless you, darling.'

When he arrived at her flat Belinda's heart was

deeply touched by his pale worried face. At first he did not want to tell her the story, but when she produced a satisfying dinner and afterwards continued to accept his refusal to speak without blaming him and continued to be gentle, loving and pathetically eager to take his mind off his troubles, he drew her to him, settled down with her in the one really comfortable armchair that would accommodate them both, kissed her in gratitude and affection, but without passion and repeated the full account he had signed a few hours before.

'It sounds like a police statement,' Belinda said, intelligently.

'It was. Word for word.'

'Oh, I see. Oh well—'

Her reddening, disconcerted face made him laugh, which did him good. Belinda hid her face on his shoulder. He lifted it away again to kiss her with considerably more warmth than usual. They continued happily this way for some time.

'I've got this devilling to do for the old man, probably for the rest of the week,' Hugh said, when Belinda moved on to the rug at his feet and sat, resting her cheek against his knee. 'But we might go out on Sunday.'

'I'm booked for the weekend at Drews Court,' Belinda said. 'Uncle John sent an SOS today. Mrs. Wood's not home yet and he's snowed under with unanswered letters. He wants me to go down on Friday evening and work them off for him.'

'Hell,' said Hugh. 'That's a bit much, isn't it? I mean, making you work off your arrears of dinner and theatres.'

'I don't think of it that way at all,' Belinda protested. 'I'm fond of Uncle John. Anyway, the balance in his favour is so large a few letters won't reduce it much. I get a weekend in the country, too, and Mrs. Heath's a wonderful cook.'

'She certainly is.'

'I expect you could come as well, if you like. Uncle John wouldn't mind. I'll tell him you can help me put the letters into good English.'

'Rash promise.'

'No, it isn't. It's your job, isn't it?'

Belinda rang up her uncle the next day. His answer was more cordial than she expected, so she relayed it at once to Hugh. If they could go down on Friday night, Sir John said, between them they ought to be able to straighten his correspondence by Saturday evening.

Hugh consulted Warrington-Reeve. He was surprised to find that he would not be needed on Saturday provided he finished his work on Friday afternoon.

'I rather thought of visiting that part of the world myself on Sunday,' Reeve told him. 'Friends want me to go down for lunch. Thought I might call on Sir John about the middle of the afternoon. He may think it a bit odd I should be in on this business of Ditchling, without getting in touch with him at all. Must do the civil thing.'

'Yes, sir,' said Hugh. He wondered what the ulterior motive was, but did not like to ask.

'Right,' said Warrington-Reeve. 'Then you'll mention the fact that I might call, will you? I suppose Miss Tollet intends to tell her uncle everything.'

'She has already. Everything she knows, that is.'

'What d'you mean?'

'I only let her know the blackmail angle yesterday evening. I said it was top secret. Oughtn't we to keep it that way? I mean, until after the inquest next week.'

'My guess is they'll adjourn again. They may take the medical evidence. The inquest on the girl was adjourned for a month, wasn't it?'

'That's right, sir.'

There was a short silence, then Warrington-Reeve said, casually, 'Is it possible to see into the bungalow sitting-room from outside?'

'See—'

'Look in, unhampered by muslin, nylon, chintz, shutters—'

'Well, yes, I should think so. You can certainly see *out*. I know – well – because I kept doing that when I was inside searching for the photo.'

'I bet you did. I suppose you can't give me a detailed list of the furniture and its various positions? And the pictures, photographs, or any other wall decorations?'

'Sorry. I know the bureau is on the right of the fireplace and there's a round table under the window. It's a long window, modern type, covers the whole side of the room looking out into the garden. That's at the side and back of the house. The length of the bungalow is at right angles to the road, if you see what I mean?'

'I shall see better on Sunday,' said Warrington-Reeve. 'Though we shall probably have the local cops to contend with. They are still trying to find the owner of the place. They are very keen. I shall rely on you and Miss Tollet to support my suggestion that we take a walk before tea – or after – if that suits Sir John better.'

Hugh promised to do his best. An expedition to the bungalow did not seem to him to offer any chance of fresh evidence, but if the old man thought it was important then it probably was.

Belinda was not quite so ready to accept the importance of every word that fell from counsel's lips, but she promised not to enlighten her uncle about the blackmail. It would only upset him further, she said. Not that he didn't know all there was to be known about the seamy side of life. His interests brought him in contact with it all the time.

'I think he wants to forget it all as much as possible,' she said. 'When I rang up to ask if you could come he said he'd be delighted. He sounded quite gay. He's rather wonderful for his age, don't you think?'

'What is his age?'

'Well, Mummy must be about fifty and he's eight years older. So he must be getting on for sixty.'

Hugh nodded gravely. The antics of these distinguished old men and women of today never failed to astonish him.

CHAPTER TWELVE

ENCOURAGED by Scotland Yard the local county police had redoubled their efforts to find out all they could about the bungalow in Neots Lane.

The land on which it was built had belonged originally to the farm farther up the lane, where Jeremy Ditchling had got his milk and eggs when he was in residence. It was unprofitable scrubland, too near the woods to turn to any useful purpose. For a time it had provided a small field of poorish grass on which a pony belonging to the farmer's children had grazed when he was not being overfed in his stable. But as the children grew up and became too big for the pony, he was sold and the land fell into disuse. When a Southfield builder offered to buy it and the local council gave permission for a bungalow to be put on the site, the farmer was only too pleased to be rid of it. His farm lay round the bend of the lane. Whatever eyesore was put up it would not be in sight of his windows.

So the bungalow was built and sold almost at once to a young Southfield couple who were tired of being on the council list for a house they could buy. But they soon found it too inconvenient and sold it at a comfortable profit to a Southfield businessman who had a friend in London looking for a weekend cottage.

Inspector Carfax had welcomed this news with enthusiasm, but found on getting in touch with the London owner that he had sold the bungalow over a year before. The sale had been made through an estate agent in Ealing. This former owner had never seen the buyer. He had simply accepted a fair price, which included the simple furniture. He had then bought a very up-to-date touring caravan.

The agent had entered into the preliminaries of the sale with a lady calling herself Mrs. Stott. With her he had travelled to see the bungalow, had gone over the details of heating, lighting and sanitation, the latter fairly primitive, the former by electricity. The sale concluded, payment had been made by a cheque drawn on the account of Henry Stott at a bank in Kilburn. Inquiries at the bank confirmed the continued existence of this account. The address of the client, which corresponded with the one given to the agent, turned out to be that of Florrie Dean. The description of Mrs. Stott given both by the estate agent and the bank cashiers also fitted. Blonde, smart clothes, heavy make-up. Undoubtedly Miss Dean.

And there the inquiry rested, much to Carfax's annoyance. Mitchell went down to see him to explain why Florrie must not be approached, at any rate for the present.

'Things are hotting up,' he said. 'We've narrowed the possibilities to four clerks – living in various suburbs of London. Inquiries are going forward, very carefully, into the private lives of these men. If one of them should turn out to be Burt we don't want him to be tipped off through Miss Dean.'

'Always supposing the insurance company theory is correct,' said Carfax, who was still feeling frustrated.

'Exactly. But it seems the most promising. One point in its favour is that none of the raids since the Wandsworth failure fits into the pattern we worked out. It looks as if Ditchling's murder had upset the organization quite seriously. Apart from Len Smithson. The two boys in that attempt have been behaving themselves up to date. The older men I saw at the Blue Boar haven't been back there since.'

Mitchell went on to put Carfax still further in the picture. This was part of the reason for his visit to Southfield and entailed some active co-operation from the inspector. The latter was obviously very keen and eager to help the case at the Southfield end. When the superintendent finished he said, intelligently, 'So what you want now is the negative of that photo?'

'Exactly. The fact that Ditchling's little camera was smashed suggests the murderer got it. But we can't be sure.'

'Took it from him by force, do you mean? In the woods? That was where the button mould was found.'

'Or brought the whole button up to London, took the camera out intact and then brought the mould down to plant it in the woods. We still don't know where he was given his lethal dose or where he was put in the car. It's possible he was drugged at the bungalow late that Thursday evening and the body disposed of in Sir John's car, *before* he went off to London airport. Young Mellanby may still be the man we want.'

Carfax agreed to this and then said, 'Any luck with the curate?'

'No. He confirms everything Mellanby said and adds nothing. I'm afraid I upset him again when I asked him if he knew where the negative was. But I'm sure he didn't know. He promised if they got at him again to come straight to us, and not pay over the money he was so thankful to get back from Mellanby. I think he will.'

'So what's the next move?'

'Keep your eye on the bungalow. See all the local agents and get them to contact you if there's a move from any quarter to buy or sell the place.'

'Right. Incidentally Miss Pope thinks one of the girls who was a friend of Mavis's knows more than she will say. Scared, she thinks.'

'I'll have a word with Miss Pope.'

Mitchell drove up to Drews Court, where he saw the headmistress at once. She could not tell him any more than Carfax had done.

'They've all been very quiet and depressed since

Mavis was found,' she said. 'The more hysterical ones have crying fits for no real reason, the others seem to have been shocked into some appreciation of reality. We are trying to use this change of mood to show them real life is a serious business and we really want to help them make a go of it if they'll let us.'

'Quite,' said Mitchell. 'Would you rather I didn't see this girl, Janet. What's she here for?'

'Care and protection,' Miss Pope answered. 'Mavis was very bad for her.'

'I can imagine that.'

'I think she must have met some of Mavis's associates. She absconded once, for thirty-six hours, but came back on her own. I think there was some sort of tie-up with Mavis's London contacts and that she suspects something or somebody. I'm afraid if you tackle her she might go off again.'

'Work on her, then,' said Mitchell. 'Let Inspector Carfax know if she comes across with any useful information.'

He drove away and as he reached the gate turned in the direction of Sir John Drewson's cottage. He had several reasons for wishing to see Sir John, not least of which was to confirm that his Jaguar, cleaned and polished and with the puncture mended, had been returned to him in satisfactory shape.

'Yes, thank you,' Sir John told him, offering a drink that he refused and a cigarette that he accepted. 'Yes. I'm not sure that I really want to keep the car. I have been out in it locally a few times, visiting my neighbours and they all say 'How can you bear to get into it?' and things like that. Or else they want to open the boot and look in.'

He shook his head over the ghoulish propensities of his friends, then asked gently if the superintendent had made much progress.

'I think we're getting on, sir,' Mitchell said. 'I think the motive for the murder, both murders, has been pretty well established.'

'Indeed?' Sir John's pale handsome face took on a look of pain and he sat for a few seconds in silence looking sadly at the superintendent.

'Since I came home,' he said at last, 'I have been trying very hard to find some explanation of the extraordinary fact that my car was used in this affair. It seems such an unbelievable coincidence.'

'That has naturally occurred to me more than once,' Mitchell told him, hoping to hear more.

'Of course I knew Ditchling was a weak character,' Sir John went on. 'You see he tried on several occasions to borrow money from me.'

'That must be a constant affliction, sir,' said Mitchell.

'Well, yes, it is. I'm accustomed to begging letters. Mrs. Wood, my secretary, deals with them. You can't start sociological projects, you know, without a lot of publicity, and then people think you must be fabulously rich and very simple.'

He smiled suddenly, a smile of great charm and modesty. 'I'm not either, you know.'

Mitchell had no answer for this, nor did Sir John seem to expect one.

'Well, I tried to convince Ditchling that temporary loans could not help him, but only regular, properly paid work. He always talked a lot about his novel, but I don't think he had much creative talent. He was clever, mind you, ingenious, full of ideas. But so disorganized. Poor boy. I'm afraid I was no help to him. I only hope my refusal to finance his wild schemes did not drive him over the edge.'

'Into criminal practice, do you mean?' asked Mitchell.

Sir John looked bewildered.

'Oh no,' he said. 'No, I didn't mean that. I meant – suicide.'

'Suicide,' repeated Mitchell, thoughtfully. The idea had been discarded by the experts long ago, but he wanted to hear Sir John's theory.

'You must know that he took various kinds of drugs,'

Sir John went on. 'He used to pull out little boxes and take pills from them quite openly when he came to see me. Like sweets, as it were. I talked to him about the dangers and evils of this habit once, but to no purpose, I'm afraid. I don't think I ever made any impression on him.'

'He went in for injections, too, when he could get them.'

'That last evening – I mean, the last time I saw him – the evening before I went to Zürich. He was in a very peculiar state. I felt sure at the time that he had been taking his pills. In fact, though I offered him a drink I suggested that it might be better for him not to take alcohol.'

'What did he say to that?'

'He was rather abusive. Accused me of being so mean I even grudged him a glass of sherry. He drank two glasses before he went away. From being over-excited when he arrived he was depressed when I saw him off into the woods. He had been telling me about his affair with Mavis, as I told you before.'

'Did you actually see him go?'

'I went to the corner of the garden, said goodbye to him and watched him take the footpath. When Hugh turned up looking for him I was surprised that Jeremy had chosen the footpath. If he was expecting a visitor I would have thought he'd use the road in order not to miss him. But his whole behaviour that evening was most strange. That's why I feel it is more than possible that he committed suicide.'

'In the woods? Then who put him into your car?'

'Himself.'

Sir John looked solemnly at Mitchell, who was too startled to reply immediately.

'They do this sort of thing sometimes, you know,' said Sir John, almost apologetically. 'Mental derangement. They want to shut themselves up in a confined space. The psychologists explain it as a sexual aberration. I think this is what may have happened to Jeremy.

He took a heavy dose of drug and then came back before it rendered him unconscious and got into the boot of my car.'

'Without anyone in this house noticing his return?'

'I was in my sitting-room again. It would be possible for him to approach from the other side and go round to the garage past the kitchen wall.'

'Wouldn't Mrs. Heath see him, then?'

'No. It was not even in the garage. It was in the drive near the garage. I had taken the ignition key out, but did not lock the car. The boot key is separate.'

'Don't you keep the car in the garage at night?'

'Usually, yes. Of course. But this particular night I was planning to leave very early the next morning. In any case I expected to take the car to the station to meet Mrs. Wood. In the end I did not do so, because she came by an earlier train. But the car was in the drive when Jeremy left and apart from passers-by in the road there would have been no onlookers for the next half-hour at least. Until Hugh arrived, I mean. Then later, when Mrs. Wood came early, just after Hugh left, I rather forgot about the car. It crossed my mind when I was going to bed that I had not moved it, but as I was going so early the next morning I didn't bother. I left it out.'

'With the key of the boot in it?'

'Yes.' Sir John smiled a little shame-facedly. 'It is also the key of the little locker on the dashboard inside the car. You will think that very wrong. Asking for trouble. Putting temptation in the way of some youngster or other. We don't have much delinquency here, apart from the poor girls at the Court. And they don't know how to drive cars. Anyway they wouldn't have a Jaguar ignition key.'

Mitchell expressed no opinion on this.

'So Ditchling could have got into the boot by himself?'

'Yes. If he did it later that night no one here would have heard him. Mrs. Heath sleeps very soundly. My bedroom window and Mrs. Wood's are on the other side of the house.'

'I see. But if he did put himself in the boot, Sir John, how did he lock himself in? The boot was locked when the car was in the pound.'

Sir John continued to gaze thoughtfully at the superintendent. He did not speak at once, then he said, 'I see your difficulty. It had not occurred to me. The boot snaps shut. I suppose whoever found the body tried it first before using the key?'

Mitchell said he did not know this, but would check.

'Yes, you had better check.' Sir John answered. 'I don't say my theory is the correct answer, but it does seem to me to be possible. If I have the opportunity I shall put it forward at the resumed inquest.'

Again Mitchell was silent. Sir John's idea had given him several of his own. Also Sir John's description of the events of that evening. Presently he said, 'Have you any theories about the girl, Miss Henning? She was not pregnant, so Ditchling's tale about getting her into trouble and wanting to marry her was poppy-cock. She may have tried to fix him that way, but I doubt if he'd take it without confirmation. Probably just another attempt on his part to get money out of you. But where does that put the girl? Rather against suicide on her part, don't you think?'

'I wonder.' Sir John looked even more drawn and sad than before. 'So young and so depraved. It is a terrible thing, isn't it? Perhaps she was really fond of Ditchling. He could have supplied her with drugs, I suppose.'

'As far as I can make out from Miss Pope who has questioned the other girls very carefully, Mavis was not particularly upset by Ditchling's death. And she was in normal good spirits when she left the school that night she disappeared.'

'I see. I thought perhaps if she was really upset she would want to follow him. Or even that he had arranged a suicide pact with her. It may be only a local rumour but Mrs. Heath tells me some traces of the pair of them were found together in the woods at the same spot.'

Mitchell remembered that the police had been followed at a respectful distance by several morbid, inquisitive onlookers and would-be helpers when the search for clues was going on.

'It's true we found a scarf of hers and something belonging to him,' he said, cautiously.

'At the same spot?'

'Yes.'

'Doesn't that suggest a suicide pact? Perhaps she flung herself in the river and he was afraid of the water or too confused by the drug and came back in a crazy state and put himself in the boot to end it all.'

'I'm afraid that won't work,' said Mitchell, 'because Mavis was wearing the scarf when she left the school some days later. She died considerably later than Ditchling.'

'Of course, of course. Stupid of me,' Sir John smiled wanly. 'I shouldn't be much good at your work, I'm afraid, superintendent.'

'All the same,' Mitchell answered, kindly, 'we haven't proved yet that it wasn't suicide. She could have dropped her scarf on her way to the river. Especially if she was a bit dopey at the time.'

'Was it on the path, then?'

'No. Not exactly. Looked like some place that had been used before.'

Sir John understood what the superintendent meant, winced and turned away his head. His next remark might have been addressed to himself.

'She went once more to a spot where she had been happy— No, it doesn't bear thinking of.'

'It doesn't sound at all like Mavis Henning,' said Mitchell, robustly. Sir John's sentimental musings sickened him. He got up to go. Sir John went with him to the road.

'I may see you at the inquest,' he said, as the super-intendent took his leave.

'I think we shall have a further adjournment,' Mitchell answered. 'There's more behind this than came your way, Sir John.'

'I'm afraid so,' the latter answered. As the car moved away he stood at the gate watching it until it disappeared round the bend of the road. Then slowly, with bent head, he walked back into the house.

Mitchell turned up Neots Lane and stopped at the bungalow. Carfax, with a police photographer, was waiting there for him. Together the three men set to work on an experiment Mitchell had arranged. When it was finished he asked for the results to be sent up to Scotland Yard as soon as possible.

'It's my belief the photo was taken in this sitting-room,' said Mitchell. 'Your film ought to prove it.'

'I hope it does,' Carfax said.

When Mitchell had gone on his way the Southfield police went back to their station. If the bungalow did turn out to be the king-pin of the case, Carfax thought, he would be delighted. In the meantime he meant to redouble his efforts to discover the real owner of the place. Surely, sooner or later, someone would want to sell it. It was a definite asset. The farmer was quite willing to buy it back for a new farmhand who had nowhere to live. Perhaps he could get an advertise-ment – but no, that would only warn off the owner if he was the criminal they wanted. Carfax decided that he must continue to be patient and carry on with routine.

Back at Scotland Yard Mitchell found a most en-couraging piece of news waiting for him.

'Lorry driver, sir,' Sergeant Jones reported. 'Picked up a girl at the river bridge on the London road out of Southfield on the night of Friday last. About ten-thirty as far as he remembers. He identifies her as Mavis Henning. Seems quite sure of it.'

'How far did he take her?'

'Right into town, sir. He put her off on Chelsea Embankment.'

'Did he?' said Mitchell, staring at the sergeant. 'Did he indeed?'

CHAPTER THIRTEEN

BELINDA and Hugh went down to Drews Cottage on Friday evening, prepared to tackle Sir John's correspondence at once and so clear some of it out of the way and perhaps win a full free afternoon for themselves on Saturday.

But this they were not allowed to do. Sir John greeted them very cheerfully, almost gaily, insisting upon immediate drinks and explaining that he had asked two of his younger neighbours in for coffee after dinner.

Hugh and Belinda expressed suitable pleasure with their arrangements, but when they were alone for a few minutes before Mrs. Heath announced that dinner was ready, Belinda said, 'Dear Uncle John. I suppose he saves up all his cash for his charities. But I don't know how he has the face to ask people to coffee, not to dinner. At his age and in his position!'

'All really successful men are a bit mean,' answered Hugh. 'That's why you must never reproach me for not being successful.'

'I like you as you are, darling,' Belinda said, with a smug, slightly possessive note in her voice.

'The maxim, I'd have you note, does not apply to women,' Hugh went on, catching at her hand.

But just then Sir John came back into the room and the conversation came to an end before it had well begun. Listening to Belinda exchanging gossip with her uncle, Hugh wondered if he would be able to have her to himself at all this weekend. His hoped-for walk, planned for the following afternoon, seemed now only a remote chance. And on Sunday Warrington-Reeve

would crash in to spoil their privacy. He remembered
that he had to make his senior's visit possible. But he
could not very well break in on the exchange of family
news, so he contented himself with watching Belinda
as she talked and wondering what Sir John would say
if he announced his recently-made decision to marry
his niece.

Dinner was a pleasant meal with Sir John continuing
to support his usual reputation for wise and witty
conversation. He told a number of amusing anecdotes
about his recent experiences in Switzerland, gave some
shrewd but not unkind sketches of his fellow sociologists
from different countries and finished up with a summary
of their conclusions and a description of their future
aims.

'We keep hoping,' he said to Hugh, with a twinkle in
his eye. 'Not like you chaps, who have given up mankind as a bad job.'

'Oh, we're not all cynics, sir,' Hugh protested. 'I'm
still capable of being surprised by some new form of
beastliness or a fresh example of unbelievable stupidity.'

Sir John sighed and then smiled, with a return of
cheerfulness.

'Linda is looking at us very disapprovingly,' he said.
'We mustn't get too serious, must we, my dear? Time
for that tomorrow, when you tackle the pile of letters
and circulars in my study.'

Belinda and Hugh exchanged glances, but said
nothing. It was clear that they would not be allowed
even to look into the study that evening.

But the next morning they settled down to their
task immediately after breakfast, first sorting, then
consulting Sir John and then settling down to the
replies, with Belinda typing and Hugh drafting the
more difficult answers and asking Sir John when snags
held them up.

By mid-morning they had reduced the pile to
reasonable proportions. By lunchtime it seemed possible
that another two hours' work would finish the job.

'I have to go out this afternoon,' Sir John said. 'If you can clear this up before tea I'll sign the lot and you can take them into Southfield to the main post office, if you will. Then they'll get to their destinations on Monday. Otherwise they won't start till tomorrow night and as they've lain here so long already—'

'That's all right.' Belinda said, ignoring Hugh's black looks. 'We'll do that, Hugh, won't we?'

'Of course,' he answered, without enthusiasm.

Sir John saw the young man's eyes turn to the window. Outside the sun was shining, lighting up the michaelmas daisies and chrysanthemums in the border and the yellowing leaves of the chestnut beyond. By teatime the sun would have nearly vanished; the best part of the day would be over.

'I think it has set fair, for another day or two at least,' Sir John said, kindly. 'Linda must show you one of our very beautiful walks, through the woods and up those hills beyond the river. You'll have the whole day free tomorrow.'

Hugh said nothing; he was still wondering how to explain about Warrington-Reeve's proposed call. Belinda came to his rescue.

'Hugh's boss is staying near here this weekend,' she said. 'He's more or less acting for Hugh over the Ditchling affair.'

'Acting?' said Sir John, interrupting her sharply.

'Well, the cops were inclined to be nasty at first, weren't they, Hugh?'

'They certainly were.' He described his first interview at Scotland Yard, but said nothing about the second one. 'I asked the old man – Warrington-Reeve – for his advice, you see,' he finished.

'Did you say he had friends in this neighbourhood?' Sir John asked. He did not seem to take Hugh's predicament very seriously.

'Apparently. He said he hoped you wouldn't mind if he called in for a few minutes on his way back to London. I said I would ask you.'

'Delighted,' said Sir John, with emphasis. 'Warring-ton-Reeve. Of course. I remember. You work in his chambers. A very famous advocate. I'd certainly like to meet him. Lawyers don't come my way much; *directly*, that is to say. Only the results of their work.'

'Hardly *their* work,' Hugh protested. 'People have to break the law or be thought to have broken it before any of us gets to work.'

'Quite right, my boy. I was only joking. What time did Mr. Reeve think he might call?'

'He didn't say. In the afternoon, I suppose. Shall I ring him up? He gave me the address.'

'Do. Ask him to have lunch with us. No, perhaps that would be inconsiderate to his hosts. Ask him to drop in for tea – or earlier if that suits him better.'

Hugh had time before lunch to ring up Warrington-Reeve, who said that he had already arranged to leave his friends in the early afternoon the next day and would therefore be passing through Southfield between half past two and three. He would be delighted to accept Sir John's kind invitation to tea.

This settled, Hugh felt more reconciled to the after-noon's work, especially when Sir John suggested that the young pair might like to see a well-reviewed film that had at last arrived at Southfield. Belinda had already seen it but Hugh had not. She had no objection to seeing it again, especially in Hugh's company. They arranged to spend the whole evening in Southfield. Both Sir John and Mrs. Heath appeared to welcome this arrangement.

The next morning the weather entirely fulfilled Sir John's prophecy. Hugh and Belinda set off soon after breakfast to visit the hills beyond the river, leaving Sir John well dug into the Sunday newspapers and Mrs. Heath happily preparing pheasant for their lunch.

During the walk Belinda said, 'Why does your boss want to come to the cottage?'

'He hasn't told me,' Hugh answered. 'But for a guess I imagine he's still intrigued by the fact that Uncle

John's car was used, while Jeremy actually lived so near. I bet he wants to look at the bungalow for one thing.'

'He could do that without going out of his way to meet Uncle John.'

'Is he going out of his way?'

Belinda turned a solemn face to him.

'Does he think Uncle John had anything to do with it?'

'With Jeremy's death? I should hope not!'

'So should I! But you aren't certain, are you?' Her voice was rising. 'There's some new evidence, isn't there? If it has anything to do with Uncle John I want to know what it is. I must know!'

'It has nothing to do with him,' Hugh declared. 'Absolutely nothing.'

'Then what is it?'

'I can't tell you more than I have.'

'But you think there may be more. Tell me.'

'I can't. Linda – darling – why start all this? I can't tell you. It involves – not only me. You know that. I can't say more than I already have.'

He took Belinda in his arms and tried to kiss away the strain and the mistrust and the anxiety she was suffering. After a time she seemed to recover and to respond to his love with the charm and happy fearlessness that had so won his heart. When they turned to walk home again she said, 'I'm sorry I was rather hysterical just now. But I simply can't bear to think of Uncle John being mixed up in a sordid crime. The car business is bad enough. He feels it dreadfully, you know. Much more than he allows himself to show. He looks ill, I think. Don't you?'

Hugh did not know Sir John well enough to have an opinion on this. Belinda's uncle always looked thin, pale and distinguished with his lined, still handsome face and his white hair and spare figure. Was he looking ill? He had never considered the matter. But he watched Sir John at lunch, noting that he ate very little and drank barely half a glass of the excellent claret that went with the meal. Perhaps Linda was right; Uncle John was ill, or worried, or both.

Warrington-Reeve drove up to the cottage in his Facel Vega at precisely half past two and in time to share the after lunch coffee and brandy. Sir John greeted him affably.

'I know the Uppinghams slightly,' he explained. 'Do you often stay with them?'

'Now and then,' Reeve answered. 'Joe and I met over Civil Defence in the war. We share an enthusiasm for golf.'

After a little more desultory conversation and while Belinda was taking away the coffee tray and helping Mrs. Heath in the kitchen, Sir John said, 'Hugh tells me you are interested in our local double tragedy – if it is local.'

'Yes. Why do you say local?'

Sir John at once embarked on the theory he had explained to Superintendent Mitchell. The barrister listened quietly.

'That's very interesting,' he said. 'And suggestive. It covers a great deal of the ground.'

'But not all?'

'No. Not all,' said Warrington-Reeve, blandly.

'The superintendent seemed to share your view,' Sir John went on. 'Of course, as a mere layman, kept in the dark as far as the police are concerned—'

He broke off, looking at Warrington-Reeve, implying that his visitor was also wilfully keeping him in the dark.

Warrington-Reeve smiled, deprecatingly.

'I'm sorry,' he said, but did nothing to expiate his fault. Instead he rose and after glancing at Hugh said, 'Would you think me very rude if I took this young man away for an hour?'

'You want to look at the woods, perhaps,' answered Sir John, calmly, 'or the river, or the bungalow?'

'Yes.'

'You will find our Southfield detectives keeping a

lynx eye on the bungalow,' Sir John smiled. 'Rumour has it the farmer wants it back but can't find the owner. Which isn't, in the circumstances, unexpected. You will take tea with us, I hope?'

'Thank you,' Warrington-Reeve answered. 'That's very kind of you.'

He and Hugh left the room together. Belinda was still in the kitchen helping Mrs. Heath to wash up so that the latter could get away for her afternoon out. In any case she had volunteered to stay with Uncle John and get tea later. The two men went out by the front door.

'The footpath,' Warrington-Reeve said, briskly.

'This way.'

With the barrister making enthusiastic remarks about the flowers and shrubs and Hugh replying, though quite out of his depth, they reached the gate into the woods, passed through and proceeded on their way. Sir John, who had watched them go from the sitting-room window, returned to his place by the fire, lay back in his armchair and went off into a light doze.

Warrington-Reeve and his escort reached the bungalow without making any stop on the way there. They found the doors locked and the curtains drawn.

'Damn,' said Warrington-Reeve.

'You didn't expect to get in, sir, did you?' Hugh asked.

'Of course not. But I expected to *see* in.'

Hugh led the way round to the back. The small window of the lavatory, half-way up the wall, appeared to be shut, but after taking a quick look round, Hugh got out a penknife, inserted it with some skill, pulled, pressing upward and the window, hinged at the side, opened outwards.

'It's warped,' he said. 'Doesn't catch properly on the inside. I found that out the first time I got in.'

'The time both the doors were open?'

Hugh grinned.

'That's right, sir.'

Warrington-Reeve also took a careful look round.

'I just want the sitting-room curtains pulled back, so that I can see into the room,' he said. 'D'you want a leg up?'

'It would be quicker, sir.'

He was inside in a matter of seconds and turned to smile down at his boss.

'Buck up,' the latter ordered. 'If the cop arrives I'll take him round the other side. You'll hear my voice. Look out while you're pulling back those curtains. It'd be a pretty tricky situation if he saw you in the act.'

But the simple deed was done, the lavatory window was closed again and the two men were standing outside the sitting-room for several minutes before they were interrupted. During that time Warrington-Reeve pointed through the glass.

'You see that big mirror on the wall on the right?'

'Yes.'

'Now look at the fireplace opposite and the bookshelves and that very tatty little table. Suggest anything?'

'I've seen them all before, of course. The furniture, I mean. I don't think I noticed the mirror. I was looking for the photograph.'

'Pity you didn't study the photograph before you left the room.'

'Why?'

'Because it was taken in there, you half-wit. And still you don't recognize the furniture?'

'The furniture in the photograph was all blurred.'

'Why was that, d'you think?'

'I can't think.'

'You are not very bright, today. If I say the order of the furniture was reversed in the photograph, does that help you?'

'I'm afraid not, sir.'

'The furniture was blurred because your photograph was the image that appeared *in the mirror*.'

Hugh stared at the mirror and at last he understood

what Warrington-Reeve meant, what Mitchell had been told by the photographic department at the Yard, what Carfax had learned when his own police photographer had made some shots in the room.

'Then whoever took it was really facing the man in the photo, with the girl's back to him,' Hugh said slowly. 'He was standing in such a position that the reflection in the mirror showed the girl's face clearly but not the man's. Then there must be another picture—'

'Of the man's face and the girl's back,' said Warrington-Reeve. 'Diabolical, wasn't it? Two birds with one photo. The blackmailer used the mirror part of his picture to attack your curate, knowing that the vital fact there was the identity of the girl, who was known to have visited him. In the other part of the picture it is the man's face, clear and identifiable that matters. He should not be embracing a girl at all. Her identity is immaterial. Double blackmail. Very profitable, if it had come off.'

'How utterly foul,' Hugh said.

A voice behind them interrupted their conversation. 'May I ask why you are trespassing on private property?'

'I told you they're keen,' Warrington-Reeve murmured. 'I wonder how much he saw.'

Turning round he explained to Carfax's man who he was, who Hugh was, where they had come from. He expressed surprise that the officer did not know of his interest in the case. All the time he was moving slowly away from the house so that the detective constable had to follow him. In the lane he would have moved away altogether, but the man stopped him.

'I'll have to ask you to prove your identity, both of you,' he said. 'I have to report all visits to the bungalow. I take it you didn't get permission to enter the grounds?'

'No,' said Warrington-Reeve, airily. 'We were simply overcome by curiosity.'

Both he and Hugh turned out their pockets to satisfy the constable, who then let them go, with a warning that they might hear more of it. As they walked away they saw him move towards a bicycle propped in the hedge outside the bungalow garden.

'He's going into Southfield,' Hugh said.

'More likely up to the farm to telephone,' Reeve answered. 'He wouldn't leave his beat for long.'

'Ought we to wait till he's gone?' Hugh asked. 'Those curtains are still drawn.'

'Dear me, so they are,' Warrington-Reeve agreed. 'No. You are not going back into that place. Far too risky. The chap doesn't seem to have noticed the curtains and if he goes off anywhere, even for a short time, he can't possibly prove it was us who pulled them back.'

'Fair enough.'

The walk back to the cottage along the road took them less time than the walk there along the footpath. Warrington-Reeve commented upon this.

'You'd think Ditchling would know the difference,' he said. 'He's supposed to have been hurrying back to the bungalow after leaving Sir John. Not only does he miss the chance of meeting you in the road, but he takes the slower route home. What does that suggest?'

'He met someone in the woods by appointment, or he was trying to avoid someone who might be on the road.'

'There's a third possibility,' said Warrington-Reeve, but he did not explain what he meant.

Sir John was still sitting by the fire when they got back. Belinda was still in the kitchen. After helping Mrs. Heath she had suddenly decided to make scones for tea and after a short rest by the fire, reading the paper and occasionally looking at her uncle's face, calm and dignified in sleep, she had gone about this task.

Hugh found her there, absorbed in cutting out her mixture ready to put in the oven. He stooped to kiss the back of her neck.

'Don't,' said Belinda sharply, concealing her pleasure. 'This isn't the flat and I'm busy.'

'To hell with that. The two old men are amusing each other.'

'Are you sure?'

Belinda, her face very pink, stooped to the oven. Hugh was aware of Warrington-Reeve, standing in the doorway.

'Forgive me, Miss Tollet,' the latter said, with deliberate formality, ignoring Hugh. 'I was looking for the garden door and opened the wrong one.'

'There isn't a garden door,' she answered. 'Or not a real one. I mean the back door is the one on the other side of the passage outside this, but it leads out to a small yard behind the garage. If you look out of the window you can see into the yard. The garden's on the other side of that fence with the climbing rose falling over the top.'

'Thank you,' said Warrington-Reeve. 'Very interesting.'

He went away, shutting the door carefully behind him.

'I know he's supposed to be brilliant,' Belinda said. 'But d'you think he's on the way downhill?'

'I should hope not,' said Hugh. 'I'm relying on him for a substantial part of my future prospects. If he packed up our chance of an early marriage would be right in the soup.'

Belinda straightened herself, looking at him severely. 'Is that a proposal?' she asked.

'It's a statement of aims. Any objection?'

'Yes. It's a lousy way of stating them. Would you mind letting me get on with the scones? I wouldn't like them to burn after all the trouble I've taken with them.'

Baffled, Hugh left her to it. Belinda, with joy in her heart, began to take out cups and saucers from the cupboard.

CHAPTER FOURTEEN

Mrs. Wood arrived at her London flat on the following Tuesday. Sir John went up to his Ebury Street home the next day and for two days they were busily engaged upon drawing up a report of his activities in Switzerland for circulation to all interested bodies.

The work was concentrated. Sir John had already spent some time during the interval between his own return and that of his secretary sorting his notes and impressions. But references had to be checked and compared with papers written by others who had attended the main conference. Mrs. Wood had to describe her own investigations of the records made after Sir John left and to correlate her findings with his. Finally the report in its complete form had to be typed and got ready for the printers.

All this kept them both busy during Mrs. Wood's working hours. There was no time to discuss other matters, even if Sir John had shown any inclination to do so, which he did not. Mrs. Wood was aware of the trouble over the car and horrified by the accounts her friends sent her, clipped from various newspapers. She expected Sir John to refer to the matter, at least to tell her the outcome. As he did neither she concluded that he had been upset more seriously than she expected and so she did not like to open the subject herself. But when on Thursday he told her he was going back to Drews Cottage the next day and would stay there probably for a week, she decided that she must find out more about what had been happening to him during her absence. Sir John had not even told her whether she was to go down to Southfield herself or in fact when he would have some more work for her. Their former pattern of activity seemed to have been broken. When she asked him about the future time-table he looked at her vaguely.

'I propose to take a short rest,' he said.

'I hope you are not feeling ill, Sir John?'

'Certainly not. I'm never ill.'

This was indeed true, for as long as she had known him. He stared at her hard as he said it, which confused her.

'I suppose I shall have letters,' he went on, almost peevishly. 'I always have letters. Linda was down last Saturday to do them for me. Perhaps you had better come, say, next Monday.'

'Very well, Sir John.'

When Mrs. Wood got back to her flat that evening she rang up Belinda and asked to see her.

'Uncle John's all right, isn't he?' the girl asked, anxiously.

'Yes. Yes, I think so.'

'You sound doubtful.'

Mrs. Wood explained her predicament.

'I think he's been very upset over Mr. Ditchling's death and the car and that. I didn't feel I could ask him, but I know so little of what happened. I thought perhaps you could tell me.'

'Well, not much,' Belinda answered, truthfully. 'Would you like to come round here or shall I come to you?'

Belinda went to Mrs. Wood's flat and told her the full story both from her own and from Hugh's point of view. She agreed with Mrs. Wood that her uncle was not quite himself, but she found this quite natural.

'I don't,' Mrs. Wood said, firmly. 'He doesn't usually get emotionally involved in other people's misfortunes, even tragedies.'

'But he *does*! He's spent his life trying to help people. Especially young people.'

'Help – yes. Impersonally. He's one of those men with high ideals who loves mankind and spends his energy devising schemes to improve their conditions.

But he doesn't take much interest in individuals. He has very few real close friends, has he?'

'He has thousands of friends!'

'Acquaintances. Can you name any permanent, intimate, close friends? I can't. I sort his letters, you know. He may keep back some but I've never seen any he doesn't want me to deal with.'

Belinda was silent. In the great pile of letters and circulars she and Hugh had coped with there had been none marked 'personal' and very few that did not begin and end formally. Among those few there was none that gave any personal, private news or comment.

'I don't know,' she said at last. 'I should have thought he cared personally about Jeremy Ditchling. I don't mean that he *liked* him. He was a horrible man, I thought. I don't see how anyone could like him. But I'm sure Uncle John wanted to help him personally. He feels the same about those girls at Drews Court. I know he does. He often goes up to discuss them with Miss Pope.'

'She's the headmistress, isn't she? I've only met her once or twice. She seemed to have a very shrewd idea about people in general. I wonder what she thinks about Sir John?'

'Admires him and is grateful for his constant help, I should imagine. Don't you admire him?'

Belinda was looking quite belligerent as she said this. All her very deep regard for her uncle showed in her fine eyes as she turned them on Mrs. Wood.

'Yes. Yes, I do,' the latter answered. 'In many ways, enormously.'

'But you're bothered about something. What?'

'I wish I knew. I mean, for certain.'

They had reached dangerous ground. Mrs. Wood felt very unsure of herself and longed for advice, but Belinda was not the person to give it to her. She decided to wait until she went to Southfield. She would talk to Miss Pope and if her disquiet was increased by an exchange of views, she would decide if she ought to come out into the open and get in touch with Hugh Mellanby or even with Mr. Warrington-Reeve.

However, in the intervening days, her resolution wavered. It was not until after she had been at Drews Cottage for three days and listened to Mrs. Heath's gossip and confidences that her anxieties returned and she left the cottage after lunch to walk up to the school.

Miss Pope, who knew Mrs. Wood slightly and for long had been a nodding acquaintance, was both pleased and puzzled by her arrival at Drews Court; pleased to get to know her better and puzzled because she had brought no message from Sir John but was there on her own account.

'I was away all through this dreadful sequence of events,' Mrs. Wood explained. 'But I did meet Mr. Ditchling once or twice and I often spend a few nights at the cottage when Sir John is working on a report or an article for the Press. I know – I mean I have seen that girl, Mavis Henning.'

'Where?'

Mrs. Wood opened her eyes wide.

'At the cottage, of course.'

'She came openly, asking to see Sir John?'

'On one occasion, yes. At least, it was in the evening – after dark—'

'When she was not supposed to be out,' said Miss Pope, grimly. 'We had a lot of that. She was never really under control. This was a most unsuitable school for her.'

'I'm sure. Well, it was after dark and I had gone into the garden to call in the cat and she came through the garden gate from the woods. I thought she was a stranger and told her where the footpath led into the road. Quite a lot of people make this mistake. Stupid, of course, because it's obviously a private garden. Perhaps not really stupid, just lazy. They see the road beyond and think it'll be a short cut and they'll get away with it.'

'What did Mavis say to that?' asked Miss Pope, getting back to the matter in hand.

'She laughed, as bold as brass, and said she'd called to see Sir John. So I had to take her in.'

'What did *he* say?'

'He wasn't angry. I mean, he didn't speak angrily. He just thanked me for bringing her in and waited for me to leave the room. She stayed about half an hour.'

Miss Pope sat looking down at her desk. Her office was well arranged and very orderly, Mrs. Wood noted, with professional interest. The average behaviour of her charges, so irresponsible, so volatile, must be a constant irritation to her, she thought. But her face was kind, serious but not severe. It was known that most of the girls respected her and some had come to like and trust her as well.

'Mavis was terrifyingly sophisticated for her age,' Miss Pope said. 'We knew she often went out in the evenings, even at night. We tried to catch her at it, but she always managed to put us off or escape our little traps and ambushes. She had her friends very well trained. They would tell us, reluctantly, that she had gone in one direction or to see such and such a person and while we were checking on this she would turn up from somewhere else, saying she had never been out at all. We knew she was lying, but we couldn't prove it. Since her death her friends have dropped a number of hints. I am positive now that she went to the bungalow on several occasions. She was quite certainly mixed up with that man, Ditchling.'

'Yes. I wonder if you could possibly give me the dates on which you knew for certain she was out? There have been times— Don't ask me why, just now. But if you could—'

Miss Pope considered. Mrs. Wood was there to discover what she could tell her about Mavis. She knew something. Why not encourage her? She could always report this conversation to Superintendent Mitchell.

Miss Pope consulted her day-books and produced

the dates in question. Mrs. Wood made a note of them.

'Did Sir John tell you that something of hers and something of Ditchling's were found in the woods at the same spot?' Miss Pope asked, when Mrs. Wood looked up again.

'Sir John hasn't told me anything. He avoids speaking about it. I think it was all a terrible shock to him.'

'I'm sure it was. It was a shock to all of us.'

'You said something of hers was found. D'you know what it was?'

'A scarf. The police brought it here to show it to me. I recognized it and the girls said she had worn it the night she left here. The last time she was seen.'

Miss Pope described the scarf, adding, as she saw Mrs. Wood's expression change and her usually healthy colour fade, 'I hope I haven't done wrong to tell you this.'

'Have you got the scarf now?' Mrs. Wood asked. 'May I see it?'

'Oh no. They've got it in London. You'd have to go to the Yard.' Miss Pope looked shrewdly at her visitor. 'You saw her wearing it, I suppose, that time she went to see Sir John?'

'No. No, I saw it later on. At the cottage. I – I must be getting back there now, Miss Pope. Thank you very much for telling me about Mavis.'

'Inspector Carfax is working on the case down here,' Miss Pope said, smoothly. 'But if I were you I'd go and see Detective-Chief-Superintendent Mitchell at Scotland Yard. He's the one that's really in charge.'

Mrs. Wood did not answer this. She merely said goodbye and walked away down the drive. She longed to go straight to London but this was impossible.

She was expected to stay where she was until after the weekend.

Sir John was in the front drive when Mrs. Wood arrived back at the cottage. He was snipping the dead heads off a climbing rose tied against the wall of the cottage near the front door.

He smiled at her as she passed him and said, conversationally, 'What had Miss Pope to say for herself? Still busy about the tragedy? Still afraid she may lose her job on account of it?'

Mrs. Wood tried to smile back. Sir John's tone had been waspish; if he was trying to be funny, it was regrettable. But she did not think he was trying to be funny. How did he know she had been to see Miss Pope? Because she came back down the Drews Court drive? He could have watched her from the drive, but not from where he now stood. She felt a small cold fear lie heavy on her breath, making her gasp a little, altering the voice in which she answered.

'I went up to say how sorry I was she has had all this trouble. I am very genuinely sorry for her. She works hard and selflessly.'

'We are all sorry for her,' Sir John said, gently, returning to his clipping. Mrs. Wood walked on into the house.

The next day Sir John said he had changed his mind about staying at the cottage over the weekend. He proposed to drive back to London on Saturday and would give Mrs. Wood a lift there if she liked. She accepted this offer with pleasure and some surprise, since her employer so often said how much he disliked taking the car to London. But she had learned from Belinda that he had hired a car to drive himself while the Jaguar was impounded, taking it out of town to the cottage and back again into London later. So she decided that Sir John's timidity operated in fits and starts to suit his convenience.

Back at her flat Mrs. Wood at once got in touch with Belinda and arranged to meet her that evening with Hugh. Her voice, with its new note of desperate urgency, impressed the girl so much that she was able to persuade Hugh of the importance of seeing Mrs. Wood and putting off their previous plans for the evening.

He arrived at Belinda's flat in a highly critical mood.

'What's the old girl want?' he demanded at once.

'How should I know? She didn't explain. But she sounded very het up. I think she may have found out something.'

'Such as?'

'Oh, don't be awkward, darling. Can't you wait to shoot her down till you hear what she has to say?'

Mrs. Wood arrived earlier than she had suggested, as if her anxiety had risen to boiling point and forced her into action; any action, so long as she did not have to keep her thoughts to herself any longer.

She began abruptly, turning to Belinda.

'Did you ever leave a scarf of yours at the cottage?'

'A *scarf*?' Belinda was too surprised to give her mind to the answer.

'Yes, a scarf. Mohair or angora. Fairly wide and long. Yellow and pink. The sort of thing girls wrap round their necks or heads with those chunky sweaters and tight jeans.'

'Definitely not,' said Belinda. 'Why?'

'Because I found one, a few months ago, at the cottage. It was tucked down the side of one of the armchairs, behind a cushion. I showed it to your uncle and he said it was yours and he'd give it back to you. It was on a Monday when you'd been down for the weekend. I've looked up the date. I wasn't there myself at the weekend, but I went down on Monday because Mrs. Heath had had to go away for a few days. Her sister was ill or something.'

'I remember,' Belinda said, beginning to get the curious story into focus. 'Mrs. Heath had a telegram on Saturday and went off straight away. But I had to get back to London on Sunday night, of course. Uncle John rang you up that evening, didn't he? He said he could manage his own breakfast for once and not to worry. He took me to the station about eight and I got a train at eight-ten. I gave him an early supper at the cottage before that and had some myself too.'

'But this wasn't your scarf?'

'Heavens, no. It sounds ghastly.'

Mrs. Wood turned to Hugh.

'Your Mr. Warrington-Reeve is advising you about the Ditchling case, isn't he?'

'Yes.'

'Then I think I ought to speak to him.'

'About a scarf that might have been mine and wasn't?' Belinda said.

'Sir John told me it was yours.'

'Then I suppose he thought it was. I'd been there for the weekend. It would be natural for him to think it was mine. He never notices what you're wearing, does he?'

Mrs. Wood's lips tightened, but she said nothing. No one ever noticed what she was wearing; they never had.

'If it wasn't Linda's, whose was it?' Hugh asked.

There was a silence, then Mrs. Wood said, slowly, 'If Sir John thought it was Belinda's, why did he never offer it to her? He told me he would give it back to her.'

Silence returned, deeper than before. Hugh got up, went to the telephone, dialled and waited. No one answered.

'Out,' he said. 'He wasn't in chambers today. Probably away for the weekend. I think you ought to speak to Superintendent Mitchell. Shall I get the Yard and find out if you can go there straight away?'

'Surely not at this time of night?' Belinda protested. She was getting tired of Mrs. Wood's mystery-mongering, as she called it to herself.

'I'd rather see Mr. Reeve first, really,' Mrs. Wood answered, looking very miserable indeed. 'He's on our side, after all, isn't he?'

'I don't think he's on any side,' Hugh said. 'I'm quite sure I'm not. Or Linda. Are you?'

'I don't know what you two mean about sides,' the girl said. 'I only know I want to save Uncle John any more bother over this whole business.'

For a second Mrs. Wood's eyes found Hugh's and
held them. Then with a gesture that might have been
anger or might have been pain he picked up the
receiver once more.

Superintendent Mitchell was still at the Yard dealing
with a back-log of reports on various cases. Mrs.
Wood's request interested him and her story fitted in
with his latest conclusions. He sent for Mavis Henning's
scarf. Mrs. Wood, when she saw it, nodded her head
sorrowfully.

'Yes, that's the one,' she said. 'I thought it must be
when Miss Pope described it to me. Particularly when
she gave me the dates Mavis was known to have been
out of the school building against the rules.'

'We shall have to check the times more closely,'
Mitchell said. 'Sir John is quite open about his interest
in these girls. He told me he has talks with them and
tries to influence them to reform.'

Mrs. Wood's face twisted into a bitter smile.

'Yes. But is a time between ten and midnight suitable, when his housekeeper is away and he is alone in
the house and the girl is breaking the rules of the
school?'

Mitchell only said, 'You have built a good deal
round the finding of this scarf at the cottage. Perhaps
your mind was already prepared and you have something else to tell me?'

'I'm afraid so.' Mrs. Wood's distress became very
evident. 'Miss Pope gave me all the dates she knew
when Mavis went out or stopped out late without leave.
On one of them the other girls say she told them she
had been to the bungalow. She boasted of her association with Jeremy Ditchling. I know for a fact that he
was *not there* on that date.'

'Were you at the cottage then?'

'Yes.'

'And Sir John?'

'Was out visiting the Uppinghams – he said.'

Mitchell looked at her, thoughtfully. Was this the

traditional deprived spinster, nourishing dirty thoughts as a consolation? But no, she was not a spinster. She had been married and lost her husband in the war. She was not attractive to look at but how many women were? And she was not enjoying this interview; she was not taking some obscure revenge; she was hating it, nervous, nearly in tears.

'You realize the implications of what you're telling me, don't you?' he said gravely.

'Only too well.' Her voice was nearly a moan and she fumbled for her handkerchief. 'But – you see – it was forced on me. Not only at Southfield.'

'Go on.'

'There was an occasion here in London. I had been typing a copy of one of his lectures that he told me he wanted urgently. I knew he was at his flat near Ebury Street, so I took it along rather late one evening. I went up in the lift and as I arrived at his landing I saw his door open and a young girl came out. He was just behind her. Of course he saw me at once. He said, 'Thank you for bringing the note from your mother. Can you work the lift? This is my secretary, Mrs. Dorothy Wood. She can take you down in the lift if you feel nervous about it.'

'Had she been there long? How d'you know she had not just delivered a note?'

'It was the way she laughed when he introduced us. She can't have been more than twelve, I should think. But her laugh – a cynical old woman of sixty.'

Mrs. Wood shuddered and blew her nose, but the tears still rolled down her cheeks.

'D'you think Sir John realized your suspicions?'

'Oh no. I don't think so. His manner to me has never changed.'

She clasped her hands, fighting to control herself.

'I ought to have left the job,' she cried. 'I wanted to, but I can't afford it. I daren't. No one wants a secretary of my age. Not to start at my age. My appearance is against me, too. I simply – daren't – leave.'

Mitchell said nothing, waiting for her to recover. Presently she said, more quietly, 'Besides, the work is fascinating. I used to consider I was extremely lucky to get the post.'

'How long, exactly, have you been working for Sir John?'

'Two years.'

Mitchell was surprised and showed it.

'Then what d'you mean by saying no one wants to employ a – middle-aged secretary?'

She flushed suddenly.

'No commercial employer does. I answered Sir John's advertisement in the *Times* personal column. I never expected to get an interview, far less the job itself. But I wanted to change. Only none of the posts I applied for would look at me.'

'Where were you before you worked for Sir John?'

She named a City firm. Then she said, more quietly, 'He really does a wonderful amount of good. Sometimes I try to persuade myself I'm wrong, having dreadful ideas, but at bottom I know I'm right. If I didn't I would never have come here. I feel like a criminal, betraying my trust, betraying my employer. I feel awful!'

'You mustn't,' Mitchell said, with emphasis. 'I'm extremely grateful to you for coming. Also I can assure you that what you have told me is not altogether news to us. Simply useful corroboration.'

Mrs. Wood began to shiver again.

'Does it mean – did he – was he—?'

'How many people know what you have told me?'

'Hugh Mellanby guesses, I think. Belinda Tollet, not. She mustn't suspect me of giving him away. She thinks the world of him. You must keep her out of it. You *must*!'

'I'll do my best. It may never be possible to prove how or why Mavis met her death. Ditchling is another story. Don't try to find out any more on your own, Mrs. Wood. Go on with your work as if nothing had happened.'

Her face grew very pale as she considered this.

'I don't think I can,' she whispered. 'I've never betrayed a confidence before. I shan't be able to face him. I don't know what to do.'

'You could always have a dose of 'flu, couldn't you?' Mitchell said. He hoped the tiresome woman was not now going to throw a spanner in the works by displaying the same scruples that had sent her to him. 'Do you have to work for Sir John again on Monday?'

'No. Not until he lets me know. He said he would let me know.'

'I see. Well, thank you, Mrs. Wood. And remember, not a word to anyone else. A lot may depend on that.'

After she had gone the superintendent took a certain number of precautions. First, he decided, he must check the various points in Mrs. Wood's story. Then Sir John was in London; he had cut short his spell at the cottage; he had put off Mrs. Wood indefinitely. It would be just as well to warn the ports and airfields and keep an eye on the Ebury Street area as well as the cottage and the bungalow.

CHAPTER FIFTEEN

THE superintendent was making progress, indeed. Inspector Hall's long, intricate and almost entirely speculative inquiries from the insurance angle had begun to pay off at last. The employees of the firm concerned had been narrowed down to three. One of these presented some curious features. On the Monday following Mrs. Wood's visit to the Yard, Inspector Hall saw Mitchell.

'Chap name of Simpkins,' he reported. 'Answers roughly to the description given by that young tearaway, Ray. Shortish, stoutish. Been with the firm ten years. Lives in New Malden. Wife. No kids. She's not very bright. Seemed quite annoyed when I asked her when I could see her husband.'

'Did she cotton on to who you were?'

'I don't think so. I said I'd come about the car. She said they'd had their Ford Popular for six years and they only used it at weekends and it was running O.K. and she was sure hubby didn't want to change it. He always went to work by train, because he used the firm's cars.'

'Is that what he tells her?'

'Apparently. She think's he's a traveller and that's why he keeps irregular hours.'

'A lot of women don't know what their husband's work really is, far less what's in the pay packet.'

'Exactly. But taken with the rest this is suggestive.'

'We'll have to tail Mr. Simpkins.'

'Yes, sir. But it won't be easy. He goes into the City in a crowd at the rush hour and he leaves in a crowd. Most days he goes up and down quite regularly. But I've missed him twice.'

Mitchell considered.

'Did Mrs. Simpkins ever see these so-called firm's cars?'

'I didn't ask her.'

'We'd better know. He did drive cars. Len Smithson confirms that. Must have hired them. We've got to confirm it.'

'Does Len know any of the makes? And dates? That'd make it a lot simpler.'

'It would. He's still in Dublin, giving no trouble at all. This thing must have been a real jolt to his type.'

Inspector Hall nodded.

'Looks like they're all marking time. Florrie Dean still lives at the Kilburn flat; she still says she hasn't seen her landlord for weeks; she still calls him Mr. Burt; and she still draws on the Stott account as Mrs. Stott.'

'Have we checked that recently?'

'Last week.'

Mitchell made a note to check again. He had a feeling that the apparent lull was part of a planned cover for action. There had been no more raids involving the insurance company where Simpkins worked; his hours of business had become strictly regular; Mr. Burt had not been seen at the Blue Boar or the flat in Kilburn. In fact Mr. Burt from being elusive had vanished into complete obscurity. Above all, Hugh Mellanby's client or friend, the curate, had not been approached again. He had not paid any blackmail. This was highly suggestive of a failure that went deep. Mellanby had taken the mirror half of the damning photograph. But it was only a print he had taken. Where was the negative? Where was the print of the other part, the part showing the face of the man who held Mavis in his greedy arms? Had this victim paid up? Had Ditchling double-crossed Burt but earned his own death in the process? Had young Mavis intervened? Bringing disaster to herself? Anyway, where was the negative now?

Superintendent Mitchell sent for Sergeant Jones.

'I want to see Mavis's old grandmother,' he said. 'The girl's clothes and other effects went to her parents, who seemed to be concerned much less about her death than the effect it would have on their own position, the bastards. Mavis took after them for utter selfishness, all right. The grandmother was the one she was fond of. It's possible she banked her ill-gotten gains with the old woman. She must have gathered quite a bit of lolly, one way or another. See if you can dig it out at grandma's.'

The next day Inspector Carfax rang up Mitchell from Southfield. He was excited and pleased.

'The bungalow has been sold,' he announced. 'Mr. Webb, that's the farmer up Neot's Lane, told me a couple of days ago he had been approached by Mrs. Stott. You remember it was Stott who bought it from the second owner?'

'Yes. Go on.'

'I asked him to advise me directly he completed the sale. He's bought it back for less than he sold the land for to the builders. He made the running entirely, I gather. Mrs. Stott agreed the transaction by telephone. He has one letter from her typewritten on a Surrey hotel note-paper. He sent his cheque to this address and asked for a receipt by return but he hasn't had one yet.'

'When was this?'

'He paid up three days ago but told me only today when the receipt didn't arrive. The whole thing was done privately – no agent.'

Mitchell thanked him and putting the receiver back, swore heartily. When he picked it up again it was to contact the bank that held the Stott account. But he guessed beforehand what he would hear. The cheque had been paid in and cashed by previous arrangement. The account had been closed. The Stotts, the manager understood, were leaving that part of London.

Mitchell swore again. The bland voice, secure in the knowledge that no details of the Stott account must be revealed, told him little more than he knew already. The farmer's delay in reporting his deal was infuriating. Probably he had been afraid of police interference. He was getting his land back at a profit with a much-needed house thrown in. He wasn't going to risk the deal not going through. At any rate it was clear the man Burt, whoever he was, was on the run. If Burt was Stott. There was one thing they could do. Pull in Florrie Dean for questioning. Perhaps he should have done this before, though it would have given away one of their main lines of investigation. No point chewing that over, now.

But Florrie Dean had gone, as Mitchell feared. They traced the Surrey hotel where she appeared to have stayed for a week. Her telephone calls to the farmer had been made from there. She had left the morning the cheque arrived. She had not gone back to her flat. Her present whereabouts could not be discovered.

Neither could those of Mr. Simpkins. He had not been seen at the office since the day the sale of the bungalow was completed. He had not gone to the flat in Kilburn. His wife had not seen him either, but she was not disturbed because, she explained to Inspector Hall, now revealed to her in his own identity, her husband's business commitments often took him away for a couple of days at a time.

'She's got a nasty shock coming to her soon,' Hall said when he reported this interview.

'In the meantime we haven't any line to follow,' Mitchell commented, grimly.

Sergeant Jones, also present in Mitchell's room, said, 'Granny Henning wouldn't open up to me, sir. She cottoned on who I was at once. Said wasn't it enough her little treasure was drowned? Hasn't the law persecuted the poor kid enough when she was alive without going on at it after she was dead? If Mavis did bank her lolly at grandma's, the old lady's keeping it, believe you me.'

'I think I'll go down and see her myself,' Mitchell said.

*　　*　　*

Warrington-Reeve was not away for the weekend, Hugh discovered. Mrs. Wood's revelations and fears had so disturbed the young man that he rang up Reeve's house again later that evening and again on Sunday morning. This time he was successful.

The barrister listened and then said, 'I've arranged to see your friend, the curate, this afternoon. Will he know the address where Mavis was living when he got mixed up with her?'

'I should think so,' Hugh answered, stiffly, annoyed by Warrington-Reeve's way of mentioning Bob's ordeal.

'Good. I'll let you know any developments. In the meantime don't discuss Mrs. Wood's lurid conclusions with Belinda.'

'That won't be easy. Why not?'

'Because she'll run off to her uncle and let all the cats out of the bag, of course.'

'I see, sir. I'll try, but I can't guarantee.'

'Take my advice,' said Warrington-Reeve, crisply. 'Practise keeping secrets from your women. Doctors do it, as a rule successfully. Lawyers should be just as careful.'

Hugh concealed his impatience, said goodbye politely and rang off. The old boy's lecture was a bore, and plainly impracticable. There was only one way of not sharing his thoughts with Belinda and that was to avoid meeting her. As he had already arranged to take her out for the day and had no intention of disappointing them both, he decided that all he could do was to pretend to share her confidence in her uncle and bring discussion to an end that way. It was a cowardly substitute for Warrington-Reeve's stern advice, but he felt it was more appropriate in dealing with his particular loved one.

Warrington-Reeve went to Bermondsey that afternoon. He found the Reverend Robert Low at the vicarage waiting for him, having just returned from taking a Sunday school class. He was shown into a small study with a wide flat table under the window, piled high with books and papers, a couple of small imitation leather covered armchairs, one or two straight-backed chairs, a bookcase reaching to the ceiling and a gas fire of which two bars did not function.

'I don't know if Hugh has explained the blackmail photo to you,' the barrister began as soon as they were both seated.

'Roughly, yes. It – it's diabolical, isn't it?'

'Criminal greed usually is. It's very ingenious, too, don't you think? Two birds with one stone.'

Bob Low was not the spineless young cleric Warrington-Reeve had expected. He was a good-looking man of about twenty-seven, with a well built, athletic body.

'Devilishly ingenious. I don't know why Hugh and I didn't spot the set-up. The furniture, even though it's indistinct, couldn't have been taken in this room, which is the only place I ever saw Mavis in, alone.'

'You are prepared to swear that?'

'Of course.'

'Did you never go to the bungalow?'

'I did once. After I'd met Ditchling. He asked me down. It was there he began to blackmail me.'

'How did you meet him in the first place?'

'Through Mavis.'

'Ah.' Warrington-Reeve began to see more clearly. Ditchling and Mavis. A useful combination. And the unknown Burt? Was he the master-mind? Who was he, anyway?

'You see,' Bob explained, 'Mavis said she had a boy-friend, a steady, and she wanted me to meet him. He was a writer, she said, too poor for them to marry straight away. I told her she was much too young to consider marriage for several years. She was, you know, by age, but not by experience and – well – physical attraction.'

Warrington-Reeve began to understand why this personable young man had succumbed so easily to a mere threat of blackmail; why he had panicked and rushed off to Hugh for help; why the latter had tried to settle the matter instead of sending him to the police. Most people would be inclined to think there was truth in the reason for the blackmail. Most people would conclude that young Low was not above sowing a wild oat or two. He himself was pretty sure, too, that the young man was not without experience.

'Where did you meet Ditchling?' he asked. 'Here?'

'Good Lord, no. Mavis suggested a pub in Notting Hill. The Blue Boar. She said Ditchling lived near there. I went and she introduced me to him. I thought he was a bit phoney – not likely to have serious inten-tions about a girl like Mavis.'

'And then?'

'Then the trouble blew up. The vicar spoke for her at the juvenile court but she had made several appear-ances there already. She was sent to the approved school. I was upset, because I'd hoped we were having some effect on her. I went to the Blue Boar on my own just after that to find Ditchling. I was lucky enough to do so. He was with another man who wasn't too pleased to see me.'

'Burt?' asked Warrington-Reeve.

'Yes. That was the name. He left almost at once. Then Ditchling told me he had taken a bungalow at Southfield and asked me down. It wasn't until I got there that he told me the approved school where Mavis had gone was quite close.'

'And then he told you he had evidence of your attempt to seduce her?'

Bob nodded. His face was flushed with renewed anger as he described the scene at the bungalow.

'I wanted to give him what he deserved right away. He was scared too, the rat. But he said if I beat him up it would double the price.'

'Did you see his evidence? Did he show you the photo?'

'Oh yes. And I took it from him and put it in the fire. He just laughed. He said the negative was in a safe place and prints were easy to make.'

'The room in the photo is the bungalow sitting-room. And the figure in the photo is not particularly like yours.'

'It's not really recognizable, is it? Nor the room? But Mavis is. That's what would count with the vicar. In any case mud always sticks. I thought I should be ruined.'

Warrington-Reeve considered for a few seconds. Then he said, 'You tell me you went twice to the Blue Boar. Would the barmaid recognize you?'

'Hardly. Well, not the first time, anyway. I went in mufti. I thought—'

'Quite.'

'The other time I deliberately went in my usual dress. A dog collar in a pub is fairly obvious. That sort of pub, particularly. But I was after Ditchling. I wanted to impress him with the fact that I had tried to help Mavis, because I was a clergyman, and that I was certain he had not.'

'I see. Now, Mr. Low, have you any ideas at all about Mavis's part in the blackmail? Was she being used without any real knowledge or was she getting her cut? Was Burt behind it all or were Ditchling and Mavis running this racket on their own?'

Bob looked thoroughly bewildered by the spate of questions. He shook his head.

'I've no idea. The only person who might know now is old Mrs. Henning, the grandmother.'

'Mrs. Henning, yes.' 'Warrington-Reeve repeated the name, in no way suggesting that this was the point he had worked towards for the last half-hour. 'Do you happen to know where she lives?'

'Of course.'

'Then perhaps you will very kindly give me her address. If you have no objection?'

'Why, certainly.'

Warrington-Reeve watched him write it down, accepted the slip of paper and rose to go.

'Will it be all right now?' Bob asked, awkwardly, as he moved to open the door for his visitor. 'I mean—'

'You mean will you be involved in any proceedings that may take place?' the barrister remarked. 'Who can say – except the police, who are investigating the double murder? It is still possible that you went to Southfield with Hugh the night before Sir John took his Jaguar to London Airport. You may have waylaid Ditchling in the woods and killed him. You and Hugh may at some time during the night have taken the body and deposited it in the boot of the car. Who can say? Obviously neither you nor Hugh is likely to do so.'

Having stunned the young man into utter silence by these remarks Warrington-Reeve said goodbye to him pleasantly and walked across the pavement to his car. Bob Low shut the front door of the vicarage slowly behind him, went back into the vicar's study and lifting the telephone receiver dialled Hugh's number.

Meanwhile Warrington-Reeve, climbing back into the seat of his Facel Vega, pulled out his map of

London and looked up the street where Mrs. Henning lived. He drew up before her door a few minutes later, passed between a double row of small boys, awed into silence by the appearance of the car, and knocked on the door. After a longish interval it was opened about four inches and a wrinkled old face peered out.

'Mrs. Henning?' Warrington-Reeve asked, politely. The answer came in a high querulous voice.

'You a copper?'

'Certainly not.'

The door was opened wider and Mrs. Henning revealed herself more fully. She was short and bent, with sparse, fluffy grey hair permed into a frizz above her lined forehead. She had dim blue eyes sunk deep in her head. She trembled a little all the time, though whether this was from agitation at his arrival or from a permanent disease the barrister did not know.

'May I come in and speak to you?' he asked, gently. 'It's to do with Mavis.'

The door began to close again.

'But I assure you I am nothing to do with the police. Quite the opposite.'

Mrs. Henning's face lit up with sudden intelligence. Warrington-Reeve found it quite startling.

'You're not Mr. Burt?' she asked, laying stress on the name.

'Why not?' he answered. It was next thing to a deliberate lie, but it could not be held against him.

Mrs. Henning opened the door wide, standing away to let him pass her. She took him into a small room at the end of the passage. It was gloomy, looking out on to a dreary backyard, but it was furnished in modern style with a bright reflecting electric fire in the grate and a television set in the corner.

'The poor lamb said I was not to speak to any but you, Mr. Burt,' she began as soon as the door of the room was shut behind her. 'She said you'd been kind enough to give 'er a good job and I ought to be grateful to you. Which I am. I'd never 'ave 'ad all this,' she waved a shaking hand round the room, 'without 'er. I loved 'er like my own child, Mr. Burt. I can't 'ardly believe she's gone. Why ever did she do it? All this in the papers. Some young good-for-nothing got 'er into trouble, I'll be bound. She was too good-natured and that's a fact.'

And too light-fingered, thought Warrington-Reeve, and too greedy and self-indulgent and neglected and spoiled and—

''Er mum and dad never did a thing for 'er,' Mrs. Henning went on. 'Never wanted 'er in the first place and told 'er so to 'er face, the poor kid. So she come to me. I give 'er all I could. She was grateful, mind you. Give me this lovely room. And now she's gone. They took 'er away from me and now she's gone.'

Tears were running down the wrinkled cheeks. Warrington-Reeve waited for the old woman to recover. Then he said, 'Mavis told you to speak to me. Will you give me her message?'

Mrs. Henning went across the room to the fireplace, picked up one of a pair of fancy vases that stood there on each side of an electric clock and tipped it up into her hand. A small package fell out, bounced on her palm and dropped to the floor. She bent down to pick it up, then replaced the vase on the mantel-piece, came back and put the package into Warrington-Reeve's hand.

'She said when you called I was to give it you,' Mrs. Henning panted. The efforts she had just made had taken away her breath.

'Did she say what it was?'

'She never told me nothing of 'er work.' The old woman began to eye him suspiciously. 'Don't you know what it is, Mr. Burt?'

'Of course. Of course,' he answered, quickly. He pulled out his wallet. Anything to take her mind off her doubts. 'Thank you, Mrs. Henning. I'm – I'm so sorry this has happened.'

He could not go on. The hypocrisy choked him. The

old woman was innocent enough; foolish, blind, but innocent and now grieving.

Mrs. Henning was not too proud to accept the notes he pressed into her hand. Perhaps she thought it was a token of appreciation of Mavis. Perhaps she just liked the sight of money. At any rate, as he intended, it brought their interview to an end.

The small boys scattered as he came out, but he saw that they had not scratched or written obscenities on the Facel Vega. Evidently they considered it a specimen of such a high order that it claimed their respect as well as their admiration.

Warrington-Reeve drove straight to his chambers, let himself into his room and locked the door. Then he opened the package. Inside several layers of paper there was a cardboard box. Inside this, buried in cotton wool, were two strips of film, one tiny, one larger. Under the cotton wool, lying flat on the floor of the box was a print. Warrington-Reeve took it out and looked at it. He drew a deep breath, put the print and the films back in the box, wrapped and tied it and deposited it in the safe in Barrett's office. Then he went back to his own room and sat down, staring out of his window at the green lawn of the Inn, at the almost bare limbs of the great elms standing there, at the pools of dull-gold leaves at their feet.

He now had the complete scheme of the blackmail. He would have to hand over his evidence to Mitchell. Must he do that without warning of any kind to all those concerned? Must he add shock to shock with added pain and confusion? Must he himself appear as the executioner or could he by delay, by occult warning, induce the real murderer to reveal himself?

Warrington-Reeve sat on in the gathering dusk of that Sunday afternoon and in the end came to no firm decision. Instead he went back to his car and drove away to the block of flats near Ebury Street where Sir John lived when he was in London. There he found the caretaker and after a conversation that raised a good many questions in the latter's mind, went on again to two separate garages in the neighbourhood. One was closed because it was Sunday. At the other he gained some useful knowledge. After that he went back to the Inn and rang up Hugh. The landlady told him Mr. Mellanby was out, but referred him to another number. He called this and Belinda answered.

'I want you both to come round to my chambers, now,' he said.

'*Now!* But we've only just got home. Hugh's here. would you like to speak to him?'

She half-turned as she spoke. Hugh, lounging in a chair at the other side of her sitting-room, grinned cheerfully. He had no intention of turning out again so soon.

'Yes, now.' Warrington-Reeve's voice took on a note of impatience. 'I have some very important and, I'm afraid, very painful news for you both. The police will have to have it, but I want you to know it first. This really is important.'

Belinda felt a sharp stab in the pit of her stomach.

'Not *another*—? Oh, not—?'

But Warrington-Reeve had rung off and Hugh had leaped across the room to fling his arms round her, demanding to know what the old man had said to frighten her like this. When she told him they stood there, staring into each other's eyes, their separate, unrelated fears turning their hearts to ice.

CHAPTER SIXTEEN

On the drive to the Inn, Hugh and Belinda spoke very little. For one thing they were both tired, after an active and pleasant day in the country together. But chiefly they were still afraid, though neither dared to give expression to the fear that consumed them both.

Warrington-Reeve greeted them briefly and led

them into Barrett's office. There he unlocked the safe, took out the package he had brought from Bermondsey, explaining as he did so how and why he had gone to old Mrs. Henning's house. Leaving the film in its cotton wool he drew out the print and showed it to the others. Hugh stared, silenced by the enormity of what he saw. Belinda gave a sharp cry of distress.

'Uncle John! It's a fake! It *must* be a fake!'

'I don't think so.'

Warrington-Reeve took the print away from her. She seemed about to tear it up in a fury.

'But it's *impossible*! Not Uncle *John*!'

Hugh said quietly, but with an indignant note in his voice, 'I suppose this is the other picture. This is Mavis's back and clearly it's Sir John's face. So it must have been taken at the bungalow. He must have gone there to meet Mavis on a day he thought Jeremy was out.'

'Yes. We can probably find out from Miss Pope if Mavis was out at a time when Jeremy was not there.'

Hugh turned to Belinda.

'There was all that guff Mrs. Wood spilled to us about a scarf. Did she go to the Yard about it? It seems to fit in with this picture, unfortunately.'

Warrington-Reeve reached for the telephone.

'If Mitchell's available I think we ought to ask him to come here and collect,' he said. 'I don't want this thing in my keeping any longer.'

'You can't!' Belinda protested. 'You *daren't* go behind Uncle John's back with that horrible fake!'

'I'm afraid I don't think it can be a fake. It was taken for purposes of blackmail, double blackmail. I'm quite certain Sir John has been approached for money. He may have paid or he may not.'

Belinda pointed a trembling finger at the print that still lay under the barrister's hand on his clerk's desk.

'It may not have been a fake as far as the photo is

concerned,' she said, vigorously. 'But don't you see, it could have been a frame-up? You can't really say from that photo whether he's trying to – to kiss her – or push her away. I'll bet any money you like she was assaulting him, not the other way round. He isn't even looking at her. He's looking up.

'His head is bent towards her.'

They all looked at the print again. Certainly the man's hands were grasping the girl's shoulders, but her body was not touching his and his eyes were looking up over her head.

'You see!' Belinda said, triumphantly. 'He isn't looking shocked or frightened. Just stern. He's caught sight of Jeremy and he's thinking, now I'll be able to get rid of this silly bitch.'

Hugh nodded, smiling doubtfully. Warrington-Reeve shook his head.

'Apart from the fact that I should hardly think Sir John would express himself, even internally, in those terms, I have more to tell you. After locking up this evidence I decided to go round to the Ebury Street flats and talk to the caretaker. I think he imagined I was connected with Sir John's welfare work and had come to see him. Sir John has gone back to the country. He went, rather unexpectedly, yesterday afternoon. He was driving himself, in the Jaguar.'

'What's suspicious in that?' exclaimed Belinda, defiantly.

'Nothing. It gave me an opening to remark about his driving habits. Though Sir John generally does not bring his own car into the centre of town, as we know, he frequently hires cars in which he drives himself, usually in the evenings. Inconspicuous cars, not new, of popular makes, as a rule. He hired a Vanguard the evening he arrived back from Switzerland.'

'I could have told you that,' said Belinda. 'He took me out to dinner and it was outside the flat. We left it there and hailed a taxi to go to the restaurant because of the business of parking. Afterwards we got another taxi and he took me back to my flat before going on home.'

'Where Mavis Henning called to see him between eleven and twelve that night.'

Belinda was too shocked to make a sound. Hugh drew in a breath and said quickly, 'The caretaker recognized her?'

'He recognized the photo of her in the newspapers after her death and he has communicated with Scotland Yard.'

'After – not before? He didn't recognize her at the time? I mean, it was the first time she had been to Sir John's flat?'

'He had not seen her before. But there were other girls, he told me.'

Belinda jumped to her feet.

'And if there were!' she cried, desperately. 'You're all wrong! Hugh, you don't believe this – this filth – do you?'

He looked at her, pale and shaken, but there was doubt in his eyes.

'*I'll* never believe it!' she said, her voice breaking on a sob. 'And you'll never prove it, either. Never!'

She made for the door. Hugh got up, too, to follow her, but she stopped him.

'I don't want you with me! Stay here and go on with your mud-slinging!'

'But Linda – darling – be reasonable!'

'*Reasonable!*' Her scorn was withering. Even Warrington-Reeve felt uncomfortable. 'When was reason any good except to mix up everything?'

'Let me drive you home. It's getting late. There won't be many buses. It's Sunday. You can't—'

'Can't get back to the flat on my own? Don't be ridiculous. I'll never let you drive me anywhere again! I never want to see you again! Oh, you're horrible – both of you!'

She was gone, leaving Hugh standing staring at the door she had shut in his face.

Warrington-Reeve put his call through to the Yard.

*　　*　　*

Mr. Burt was worried. He was also angry, when he should have been resigned. After all, he had done exceptionally well. He had a tidy little fortune salted down in various parts of the world and a nice comfortable sum in cash to start him off in some other country, preferably one where Interpol did not operate and where money could stave off extradition. He had no right to be dissatisfied.

But he was. Failure had always particularly distressed him. Two failures in line, putting an end to his pleasantly exciting double life seemed to him the darkest tragedy. It was so unfair. He, who always thought of everything, who had always dominated the boys who worked for him, to be out-smarted by a pair of juveniles. It not only put him in peril, forced him to pull out, it was humiliating. He could not endure to be humiliated.

Besides, Mr. Burt was not living comfortably at this time. He dared not go home; the cops had been at his wife, though they had so far made no other move. He could not go to the office; they had been there too and he had had a nasty time throwing off the man who had tailed him on his last appearance with the firm. He had spent three days moving from one seedy commercial hotel to another, avoiding all his usual pubs, not communicating with anyone while he made his final preparations to leave.

And still the thought of failure nagged at him. Also the loss of that useful thousand pounds young Jimmy Dice had done him out of. He had underestimated Mavis, too. That was the trouble. Such a kid. But a deep one. It really rather shocked him to consider the depths of her depravity.

Jimmy must have given her the film, to keep it from him, but what had she done with it? Tried to pull off the job on her own? Sold it to the old man? In that case there was no point trying anything now. Better to go while the going was still fairly safe. But there was still that duplicate print. Could he stand not cashing in on that?

Mr. Burt got out the print and looked at it. Photographically it was fine; young Jimmy certainly knew his stuff. He'd had a good deal of experience, of course, before he himself had teamed up with him. That was the snag, unfortunately. Jimmy was brilliant but unreliable. Unbalanced, really. He couldn't take direction. Not even the direction of genius that he was offered.

Into Mr. Burt's musings there crept a note of urgency. No good crying over spilt milk. Must mop it up if possible. How? Think out what Mavis could have done with that film. It was certain she'd gone up to the old man's flat. Taken it with her? Not she. Far too cagey. Then where?

Mr. Burt exclaimed aloud, instantly clapping his hand to his mouth and swinging round to face every side of the drab hotel room as if he expected half a dozen police faces to pop out from the tall wardrobe, from under the bed, from behind the heavy chest of drawers. But the room was empty, no heavy footsteps approached the door, his revelation was not shared.

Carefully putting his respectable bowler hat on his head Mr. Burt went out. The Sunday streets were as empty as his room. He arrived at Mrs. Henning's door in Bermondsey just after six o'clock and knocked. As always she opened it a few inches to peer out.

'Can I come in?' he said, politely, and added with suitable gravity, 'I want to speak to you about poor little Mavis. I knew her, you know.'

Mrs. Henning did not know. On the other hand she was aware of Mavis's very wide range of friendships. She repeated her usual caution.

'You a copper?'

'Certainly not.' Mr. Burt was genuinely shocked by the suggestion.

She let him come in, led him to the smart little sitting-room that Mavis had furnished for her and remained standing, waiting for him to disclose his business with her. Her silence disconcerted the visitor.

'I've come to ask you about Mavis's – er – assets,' he began, awkwardly.

''Er what?'

'The things that belonged to her. Valuables – and so on.'

'What's they got to do with you?'

He decided to come to the point, brutally if need be, otherwise they'd go on like this all night.

'Mavis had something of mine in her possession that was not found with her when she – died. I thought she might have left it here with you.'

The old woman looked puzzled.

'Don't know of nothing,' she said. ' 'Cept that parcel she said to give to Mr. Burt when he called.'

His spirits soared. He had maligned the poor kid. She'd only been keeping it from Jimmy. Or perhaps, he thought, cynically, she thought he'd buy it at a higher price.

But he smiled at Mrs. Henning, held out his hand and said simply, 'That's fine. You can give it to me. I'm Mr. Burt.'

The old woman was scandalized.

'Well, of all the—Mr. Burt come for it 'isself only this very afternoon. Couple of hours since, it was. I don't know 'oo you may be, but you can take yourself off this minute. Mr. Burt, indeed! Mr. Burt was a *real* gentleman, gentleman's coat, no 'at, white 'air, posh car. My Mavis knew class when she see it. Get along with you!'

Mr. Burt, mortified beyond words, had no reason to think she was not speaking the truth. Then who was the interloper who had stolen this march on him? The answer was obvious. Drewson himself, the cunning old fox. Drewson, who was at the bottom of all his misfortunes, who had brought him to the position he was now in!

Mr. Burt hurried away from Bermondsey. At Victoria station he went into a public call box and dialled a number.

'Doll?'

'Yes.'

'This is it.'

He explained the situation in guarded tones.

'I've still got one print. I'm going to use it on him.'

'Is that sensible?'

'Listen.'

He detailed the rest of his plan.

'So you've got to come with me, Doll. I've had the tickets and passports for weeks. Chapman, we are now. Mr. and Mrs. Chapman. Gatwick to Jersey. Local steamer to St. Malo. Train to Lisbon. It'll be slow with the changes, but safer. Fly on to—'

'Don't. I'm getting too excited. Tell me again what I have to do.'

Slowly, carefully, Mr. Burt gave her his instructions.

*   *   *

When Inspector Hall rang him up at his home, Superintendent Mitchell was on the point of going to bed, early for once. Fortunately he had not yet got very far with his undressing. He merely had to put back the coins and other objects he had just taken from his trouser pockets, replace his tie and pull on his jacket.

His wife watched him from the bed where she was already comfortably settled.

'Not again!' she exclaimed.

''Fraid so. This looks like *it*, as far as one case is concerned.'

'The Ditchling murder?'

He went over to the bed, stooped and kissed her. 'That's asking,' he said, firmly.

Mrs. Mitchell sighed. It was no fun being married

to a policeman, as she always told those who said they envied her. You had to wait for it to come out in the papers, just like anyone else.

'Well, Frank?' Mitchell said when he reached the Yard. 'This is it, I should think.'

'It might be, sir,' Inspector Hall replied, cautiously.

'Where are they?'

'In your room.'

'I shall give them the news from Drews Court and Len's latest contribution. But I don't think I'll mention Florrie Dean. It doesn't concern them.'

'You mean her turning out not to be Mrs. Stott?'

'And all that implies. Yes.' Mitchell took a turn up and down the room. 'You're dead sure now it wasn't Florrie?'

'Absolutely, sir. I took Florrie's photo round to the bank manager and the hotel manager in Surrey. They were quite definite there was no real resemblance. The photo was black and white. Without the colouring, as described, and the clothes, that put us off before.'

'Quite. They were assumed for that purpose. You were meant to think she was Florrie.'

Inspector Hall looked at his chief with respect.

'When did you cotton on, sir? I mean, ordering that photo of Florrie. She didn't suspect a thing – till afterwards.'

'Transistors are a great help,' said Mitchell, not answering the question directly. 'Where's Florrie now, by the way?'

'In Brighton. Not much of a place for her, in the winter, I shouldn't think. Would you, sir?'

But Mitchell had already reached the door and this question, too, went unanswered.

Back in his own room, with Warrington-Reeve and Hugh sitting opposite, Mitchell stared down at the print of Sir John and Mavis. The box with the films lay beside him on his desk.

So this slick barrister had succeeded where Jones had inevitably failed. It had been stupid to send a cop down to see Mrs. Henning. Of course the old woman wasn't as simple as all that.

'This clears up the whole blackmail, doesn't it?' Warrington-Reeve said, when the superintendent showed no signs of speaking.

'It certainly does.'

Warrington-Reeve described the rest of his researches, adding, 'But you probably got the same facts out of the caretaker and garages'.

'We did. We also found that Mavis hitched to London that night on a lorry that put her down on the Embankment in Chelsea. A short walk to Ebury Street. We have also had a report from Miss Pope. A girl called Janet, a friend of Mavis's, has confessed that Mavis told her about the blackmail attempt on Sir John. Mavis thought it a huge joke. She couldn't keep the secret of how the photo was taken.'

'Did her description tally with what we have been forced to suspect about Sir John?' asked Warrington-Reeve, stiffly.

'It was not concerned with that aspect of the case. But Janet said, according to Miss Pope, that dirty old men deserved everything that was coming to them.'

'Then we haven't much choice,' said the barrister. 'Sir John was being blackmailed in a peculiarly deadly fashion. Any publicity would destroy not only his own reputation, which he has been so very careful to preserve, but his public work, which would become a subject of derision, more withering still. He had to act, and as far as Ditchling is concerned I can hardly find it in my heart to blame him.'

'It all fits in,' said Hugh, with something like a groan, 'I suppose Jeremy never left the cottage at all that night, in spite of what Mrs. Heath said?'

'She couldn't actually see them from the kitchen,' Warrington-Reeve went on. 'She could only hear voices.'

'That's so,' Mitchell agreed.

'Sir John must have put the dope into those sherries

he gave Ditchling. Before he actually passed out he helped him outside the house, made his remark in a loud voice for Mrs. Heath's benefit, led Ditchling to the car standing in the drive, opened the boot, made some pretext for getting the drowsy blackmailer to look into it and tipped him inside. It would be quite easy even for a man of Sir John's frail physique, especially with an unresisting victim. He locked the boot and went into the house, intending to leave rather early in order to fetch Mrs. Wood from the station and dispose of the body in the river or in the woods, before going into Southfield. There are several rough tracks among the trees or along the river bank where cars park for picnicking. He could have backed into one of them quite easily. It was dark by then, remember.'

'But he was interrupted,' said Mitchell, who found the barrister's story rather too detailed.

'Exactly. First by Hugh and then by Mrs. Wood's unexpected arrival in a taxi. He was completely stymied. Daren't take the car out again. Couldn't dispose of the body any other way. So he left it – had to leave it – hoping to carry out his former plan on his return.'

'Linda was left to bring down the Jag with a murdered body in it!' exclaimed Hugh, in horror.

'He daren't alter the arrangement with her, either,' Warrington-Reeve said. 'But when the body turned up in the pound it is significant that he changed his immediate plans and stayed in Switzerland to see how much would break immediately. I suppose he decided it was safe to come home.'

'He told me he'd made up his mind it was suicide,' Mitchell explained Sir John's theory.

'Cunning old devil!' Hugh broke in. 'Mavis's death put paid to that!'

'Oh, no. Not necessarily. It was out of character, but we had to consider it until – other facts emerged.'

Warrington-Reeve had been thinking rapidly.

'Sir John is responsible for her death, too, I imagine? We know now that she went to London to see him on the night he arrived back. We know that Ditchling had given her the film to look after and she parked it, as she thought safely, with her grandmother. Must have done this some time between Ditchling's last blackmail attempt and the discovery of his death, because it would seem she went straight up to Ebury Street the last time she was seen alive.'

'He gave her the same treatment,' Hugh said. 'Drugged her, took her down to Southfield, tipped her in the river and drove back to London. It wouldn't take him more than a few hours to do the round trip.'

'Then he went down to the cottage early the next morning,' Warrington-Reeve resumed. 'At some time after that he planted Mavis's scarf and Jeremy's button, out of which he had taken the camera, in the woods, just to confuse the issue.'

Mitchell sighed. He put the print back in the box, together with the films and gave them to Sergeant Jones, who had been listening with astonishment to the two barristers, nattering away without a word from the chief to stop them.

'Get these entered and locked up,' Mitchell ordered.

'Yes, sir.'

The superintendent turned to the others.

'You've worked it out pretty much as I did,' he said. 'But there's one thing worried me from the start. Too much coincidence. I don't like coincidence. It isn't natural. I always try to break it.'

'What coincidence?' asked Warrington-Reeve.

'Ditchling going to live at Southfield, for a start. A blackmailer settling down near the victim quite a time – a year wasn't it – before the blackmail is worked out. Was he prospecting or was it a plan? If so, how did he know Sir John was a likely subject?'

'That could be my fault,' Hugh said. 'I saw him once or twice and I had no idea what he was doing. I'm afraid I talked to him quite freely about Sir John and his good works.'

'But that would be *after* he went to the bungalow, wouldn't it?'

'Yes. Yes, I suppose it would.'

'There's a man called Burt,' said Mitchell, carefully, 'Yes, the one whose name you took, Mr. Reeve. He's done some pretty well-planned jobs in the last few years. He plans very carefully, – detailed recce, everything worked out to the second.'

'That raid,' exclaimed Hugh. 'The one that failed and you—'

Mitchell nodded.

'Oh yes, you were on to that, Mr. Mellanby.'

'Burt,' said Warrington-Reeve. 'The boss who was being double-crossed by Ditchling and the girl.'

'We think we've got him on the run,' Mitchell said. 'I can tell you now that I've had another piece of information from the man who drove the Jaguar away from the airport.'

'You know who that was?' exclaimed Hugh.

'We've known from the start. He's an old friend of ours. He now says, and I've no reason to doubt his word, that he was ordered by Burt to take the Jag. He was told the number of the car and the number of the ignition key, so that he could drive it away. He was told the time he could pick it up and it was impressed on him not to be late because someone else was detailed to take it away from the airport. He was told to deliver the car, after the raid, and after he'd dropped the rest of the gang, at a certain place and there leave it locked up. He says he did not report to Burt he'd taken the car; it wasn't necessary, because the rest of the gang had been briefed to expect a Jag. You see what I mean about coincidences, Mr. Reeve? How did the gang know to expect a Jag unless Burt told them *in advance* of its theft? Len's new statement explains a lot more, doesn't it? It also explains why he shot off to Ireland when he got to know what he'd had in the boot of the car. I think he's speaking the truth when he says it was a shock to him.'

'Then the body *was* put in at Southfield?'

'Oh, yes, I think so.'

Hugh was appalled.

'But that means that Sir John – and this Burt—'
He turned to Warrington-Reeve. 'Linda!'

Mitchell said, sternly, 'What's all this?'

'Miss Tollet,' Warrington-Reeve said, quickly. 'We
thought it best to break the news about her uncle. We
showed her the photograph.'

'She was furious,' Hugh cried. 'Can I use your phone?
She must be told more. She must be told not to—'

Mitchell put him on an outside line. At Belinda's
flat one of the other girls answered. Hugh put down the
receiver: his face was white and strained.

'Betty says she rushed in, packed a bag and said she
was going down to the cottage immediately. She had
just time to catch the last train. She got a taxi.'

Mitchell went into immediate and astonishingly
swift action. In a very short time a small posse left
New Scotland Yard. The Facel Vega was in the lead
with Mitchell and Hugh. Warrington-Reeve was at
the wheel. Behind came a police car with three men
in it, including Inspector Hall and Sergeant Jones.

As they swept through the quiet night streets of
south London Mitchell explained the most important
coincidence of all; that explained by the existence of a
Mrs. Stott, who had turned out not to be Florrie
Dean.

CHAPTER SEVENTEEN

Sɪʀ Jᴏʜɴ was in his sitting-room at Drews Cottage
when the front-door bell rang. He got up at once to
answer it, meeting Mrs. Wood in the hall.

'Better put another cup on the tray,' he said. 'I
think I know who my visitor is.'

Mrs. Wood retreated into the kitchen where the

coffee was already bubbling in the percolator. Sir John opened the front door.

'I thought it might be you,' he said. 'I suppose you want to speak to me.'

'You thought right,' Mr. Burt said, with an air of insolence.

'Very well. There is no point in your coming in but I know I can't prevent it.'

He turned away, leaving the door open and went back to his place by the fire, leaving Mr. Burt to enter, close the door and follow him into the sitting-room. Sir John's rudeness had been more telling than Mr. Burt's. The latter's face showed mortification; Sir John was calm.

'Seeing you made no attempt to meet my very moderate terms—' Burt began in an angry bluster.

He was checked by the other's upraised hand.

'Quietly, please. My secretary is making coffee. I shouldn't like her to hear you.'

'I'll bet you wouldn't.'

Burt looked round, but the door he had closed behind him was still shut and he was alone with his victim. Before he could go on with his attack, Sir John said, quietly, 'There is no need for me to meet your terms. Your threats mean nothing, now. You have lost your proof and my word is quite sufficient to put you in prison for a long stretch. Quite apart from any more serious charge.'

Anger surged through Mr. Burt, making speech impossible. So it *was* Drewson who had got hold of the film from Mrs. Henning. What had she said? White-haired. A real gentleman. Well, here he was, with his buttoned-up face and his thin lips and frosty eyes. A real gentleman, was he?

Mr. Burt was working himself into such a fury that Sir John became alarmed for his own physical safety. He decided to explain himself more fully.

'When my niece rang me up an hour or two ago to tell me she knew about your blackmail attempt because Warrington-Reeve had taken possession of the film—'

'What's that? Warrington—? Who—?'

'Mr. Warrington-Reeve, whose name I'm sure you know. It is very well known in the criminal world.'

Mr. Burt's face, which had turned very pale now reddened again.

'You can pass up those cheap cracks, Drewson,' he said. 'Are you telling me it wasn't you took the film from Mrs. Henning?'

'I don't even know who Mrs. Henning is. Poor Mavis's mother, I suppose? Or the grandmother she used to speak about?'

He was telling the truth, Burt decided. Common sense urged him to give up, while he still had time. If the girl knew about the film and that lawyer chap, who was a holy terror, then by now – by *now* – the cops were on to it, too. At any minute—

He moved to the window quickly and parting the curtains looked out. It was a dark night, no moon; no stars. In the short gleam from the window he could see the lawn, but the drive was round the corner, hidden. Was his car all right? Was it still there? Was the drive empty, or were there figures, silent dark-clad figures, creeping slowly towards the house? He must go. He knew he must go.

'I have not warned the local police yet,' Sir John's voice came from behind him, directly behind.

Burt dropped the curtain, began to turn, but two hands, uncommonly strong hands, took his arms, twisted them behind his back and held him pinioned.

'Mrs. Wood!' called Sir John, with a note of triumph in his voice. 'Will you come here at once, please.'

She was at that moment bringing in the tray with the coffee. To Sir John's horror she gave a little laugh as she put it down.

'Mrs. Wood,' said Sir John, subduing the disagreeable effect of that laugh. 'Please ring up Inspector Carfax and ask him to come here at once.'

'Doll,' said Mr. Burt, 'bash the old b— for me. He's hurting me.'

Mrs. Wood came closer. She was still laughing.

'You don't know how comic you look, the pair of you,' she said. 'Why don't you drop this nonsense, Sir John, and have your coffee? We won't detain you long, will we, Harry?'

Sir John's fingers lost their grip. He felt stunned and sick. He moved away, stumbling a little and sat down in his chair, drawing it closer to the fire as he did so, for he was suddenly very cold.

'That's better,' said Mrs. Wood, briskly, holding out a cup to him. 'It's your own fault it's come as a bit of a shock to you. You shouldn't have gone for Harry.'

'No,' said Sir John, heavily. He leaned forward to take his cup and put it down in the hearth beside him. Then he pulled forward a basket of logs to throw one on the already glowing fire. 'No,' he repeated. 'I see that now. Also I should not have sent for you when Mrs. Heath was called away again this evening.' He paused, then added, 'But that was intended, I suppose? The call to her was a hoax. Her sister has not had a relapse?'

'Of course not,' Mrs. Wood said, cheerfully. 'We wanted Mrs. Heath out of the way and I knew you'd never try to manage on your own. As Harry said, he'll call you at once and you can go down by train and I'll pick you up at the cottage when I'm through with him. Didn't you, Harry?'

Mr. Burt grunted assent.

'Come to depend on me, haven't you?' Mrs. Wood went on. 'Harry said I could do it – make you depend on me, I mean.'

Sir John took a sip of his coffee. He felt he needed it. For two years he had worked with Mrs Wood, liked her, trusted her. Never for a moment suspected her. And all the time she had been betraying him with this man. And he thought himself so clever with people, summing them up. It galled him particularly to remember how

he had taken Mrs. Heath to the station so that he
could meet Mrs. Wood's train and bring her out to the
cottage. It fitted so nicely with a quiet dinner in
Southfield. And now this.

He thought again of Mrs. Heath. Surely when she
arrived and found out that her sister had not suffered
a relapse at all she would have got in touch with him?
Or started straight back?

'Mrs. Heath—' he began.

'Not likely to start straight back,' Mrs. Wood told
him. 'Even if there was a train which there isn't.'

'She'll be back first thing in the morning.'

'That's right.' Sir John caught a quick glance she
gave Mr. Burt at this moment. He began to know the
true meaning of fear.

With a hand that shook he lifted his cup once more.
He was helpless and he knew it. His only chance was
to keep them talking until Scotland Yard, who by now
knew all, took action.

'I came down here to sell you that film,' Mr. Burt
persisted.

He was all on edge now, but his greed still drove him.
'You got the money ready for me, didn't you? *Didn't
you?*'

'You no longer have the film,' Sir John said, faintly.
He was beginning to feel very tired, too tired to care
much what happened now, so long as this pair of
vultures would go. He saw Mrs. Wood's eyes upon him,
lifted his coffee cup again, choked a little and turning
towards the fire, got out his handkerchief to cough into.

'But I have a print,' Burt said, taking it from his
wallet. 'It may be the last, but it's just as deadly if I
plant it in the right place, isn't it?'

'Isn't what?' said Sir John, thickly.

'Buck up!' Mrs. Wood admonished. 'I don't know
where he keeps his dough and he'll be off any minute
now.'

Sir John heard them, through the mists that eddied
in his mind, lifting and falling. His life work depended

on his reputation. His reputation must be saved, at any cost. The police would not destroy it. Or would they? This man and woman, these two snakes, were vindictive, pitiless. If only they would go.

Burt and Mrs. Wood watched him. He was swaying to and fro in his chair, his eyes closing and opening, his head drooping forward.

With what appeared to be a desperate effort, a last gathering of his fading strength, he muttered a few directions to Mrs. Wood.

'What's he say? Where is it?' Burt demanded. 'Can you make out—?'

'I can.'

Efficiently, as always, Mrs. Wood took the keys from Sir John's wavering fingers, unlocked the drawer in his desk where the notes lay in neat bundles and halving the bundles gave Burt his share and stowed her own in the suitcase she had put down outside the sitting-room door.

Mr. Burt watched her without speaking. Let her think she ruled the roost at this moment. She'd know better later on. Just now there was no time for argument.

Mrs. Wood slipped the key back into Sir John's pocket. He lay awkwardly in his chair, his head fallen now to one side, his eyes closed, snoring with a strangling sound. She moved his head into a better position, propping it up with a cushion. The snoring stopped.

'Come on!' Burt urged. 'Leave the old bastard. He's all right, isn't he? What does it matter how he's found?'

'Suicides always make themselves comfortable,' Mrs. Wood said calmly.

'Never mind that. Time's getting on. We don't want interference.'

'Young Tollet, you mean? In case she comes down?'

'You heard him, or didn't you? She rang him up. They got the film. Of course she'll come down. To-night.'

'Trust me to know the times of trains. And there won't be any taxis. Not unless she rings up for one.'

With these confident remarks Mrs. Wood picked up her bag and followed Mr. Burt out to the car.

*   *   *

Belinda travelled down to Southfield with a mind relieved by a short conversation with Sir John on the telephone. There had been just time to make her call before her train left. She was naturally surprised to hear that Mrs. Wood was at the cottage since she had understood that her uncle was resting and his secretary staying at her flat in London. She was sorry for Mrs. Heath, who never liked travel and must be suffering all this fresh anxiety due to the relapse of her sister's illness. She had to interrupt Sir John to give him her message about the blackmail. Once she started he did not stop her but heard her out. Then there was silence. She had to ask him if he had heard her. She stammered a sort of apology. He simply thanked her and rang off. He did not seem upset. Not at all as if he were guilty of – well, of anything.

But in spite of Uncle John's calm and her own confidence in Mrs. Wood's efficiency she wanted to reach Drews Cottage as quickly as possible. She, too, knew that taxis did not as a rule wait at Southfield station for the last train. Certainly there would be none on Sunday. She could ring up for one from the station, but that would waste time, another half-hour probably. Or she could hitch – less certain, more time-wasting if it failed.

When the train reached Southfield she had still not decided what to do. But for once luck favoured her. As she was looking round the station approach to make sure it was empty a car drove up. She ran to it.

'Sorry, miss,' the driver said. 'Ordered in advance.'

The passenger, a youngish man, with a pleasant voice, came up. Belinda explained her need, begged to share the taxi. The driver agreed, only refusing to go out of his way on the journey.

'That's all right,' Belinda said, cheerfully and told him where he could drop her, about a quarter of a mile from the cottage.

So it came about that she arrived there a few minutes before Mr. Burt and Mrs. Wood left the house. They were so intent on their final preparations that they did not hear her footsteps in the drive.

Seeing the light from the sitting-room window shining on the lawn at the side of the house, Belinda began to feel remorse for keeping the household up so late. But when she made out the shape of a strange car in the drive she checked in sudden alarm. Was it a police car? So soon. Was she too late?

She could see very little but she had been walking in the dark and her eyes were becoming accustomed to it. She could make out that the car was not a police car. Also it was unlocked She opened the door, felt about and found the light switch. Certainly it was not a police car. Then whose?

Switching off the light, she shut the door again without slamming it. It could belong to friends; it was much more likely to belong to enemies. In which case to walk boldly into the cottage would do no good to anyone.

Praying that the back door was unlocked, Belinda crept along to it. The handle turned, she was inside, in complete darkness, breathing fast.

But she knew her way about this house. Without putting on any light she found the kitchen door and began to open it. There was no light on in the hall, but the sitting-room door was open and she heard, with increasing shock and horror, the final words spoken between the criminal pair. A few seconds later she heard them pass out of the front door, shutting it behind them.

It was only then that she lost her head. If she had waited until she heard the car leave the drive she would

have had all the time in the world at her disposal, un-
disturbed. But her mind was filled with her uncle's plight,
his immediate dreadful peril. Or his death? In either
case she must get to the telephone, to summon help or
organize pursuit or both.

She went swiftly into the sitting-room, stumbling
against a chair as she did so. Sir John, unmoving, pale,
was breathing still. The ambulance, then, first. She
dialled 999.

Outside in the drive Burt was sitting at the wheel, the
engine of the car running smoothly. Mrs. Wood, her
hand on the door at the opposite side, stooping to get
in, straightened suddenly.

'He's come round,' she said.

'You're crazy. Get in, for God's sake. We'll miss that
boat.'

'He's come round and he's on the phone,' Mrs. Wood
insisted. 'I'm going back to see—'

'Get in, you silly cow!' Burt shouted. 'Or I'll go
without you.'

But Mrs. Wood was halfway back to the front door
and cursing under his breath Burt climbed out and
followed her.

'Ambulance?' cried Belinda, forgetting to lower her
voice, forgetting everything except the sight of her
beloved uncle so still, fading from life before her eyes.
'Sir John Drewson, Drews Cottage. He's been poi-
soned—'

She saw Mrs. Wood burst in, eyes staring, mouth
open in screaming rage. 'Police, too!' she yelled.
'Police—'

The receiver was torn from her hand. She ducked
her head to one side to avoid Mrs. Wood's clenched
fist but felt a harder blow on her shoulder. Half-
fainting from pain and terror she felt herself bundled
out of the house and pushed into the back of the
waiting car. The engine was still running. In the next
instant the car had left the drive and roared off into
the night.

CHAPTER EIGHTEEN

INSPECTOR CARFAX, eagerly acting upon Superintendent Mitchell's latest information, decided to set up
up road blocks on every exit from Southfield, including
the railway, before he went in person to Drews Cottage
to make, he hoped, the key arrest in the case. It took
him some time to organize this scheme, but he had no
reason to suppose that the criminals had been warned
of their imminent danger and he dared not risk arriving
at the cottage to find it empty.

So when the Facel Vega swept down the straight
half-mile approach to the river bridge on the London
road, Warrington-Reeve saw ahead the red lights of
the road block and came to a halt a few yards from it
quite smoothly but with such a sudden reduction of
speed that all three men felt their safety belts cut into
them sharply.

'Ouch!' Hugh said. 'That got me where it hurt.'

'Be thankful you aren't picking the windscreen out
of your face,' Warrington-Reeve told him.

They climbed a little stiffly out of the car. Mitchell
went forward to the road block where a sergeant
explained Carfax's orders. The superintendent nodded.

'Had anything through?' he asked.

'Couple of lorries, sir. We searched them but they
were O.K.'

'They'll be in a car if they come this way at all,'
Mitchell told them.

'There's a car on the road now,' Hugh said, moving
clear of the bridge on to the sloping verge that ran
down along the junction of the side road, separating
it from the river bank. This side road was the end of
Neots Lane, where it joined the London road again
after passing the farm.

All the men listened. The sound of the car was

distinct but it was difficult to decide whether it was in
the lane or on the main road. At any rate it was coming
from the direction of Drews Cottage and it was moving
fast.

It appeared from round the bend of the main road,
half a mile away, headlights undipped. The red lights
of the road block must be entirely obvious, Mitchell
knew, but the car seemed to increase speed rather than
check it. This was madness. If it wasn't some fool
driver, half-asleep, it must be their quarry.

'Get ready to jump for it!' he yelled to the men near
the block. 'The bridge'll wreck him if he crashes the
block!'

But Burt had other ideas. He had seen the block as
he rounded the bend and rightly interpreted its
purpose. But he knew the junction with Neots Lane.
He decided to swing back into it and make for the
London road again at the other end. It would mean
passing through Southfield, but it was, after all, the
right way to get to the west. He had only started in an
easterly direction to avoid the built-up area where
cops on the beat might notice the number of his car. He
had meant to leave the London road as soon as possible
and make a wide circle of the town.

It took him only a couple of seconds to change his
plan. But it meant driving almost up to the bridge
before he swung off down Neots Lane. Beside him Mrs.
Wood was rapidly reaching hysteria.

'It's a road block!' she screamed, suddenly. 'Stop!
You'll have to stop!'

He did not speak. His whole mind was on the turn.
They were nearly there; he could see figures darting
away from the centre of the road.

'Are you mad!' Mrs. Wood yelled. She clutched at
his arm. The car swerved and rocked but he shook her
off, regaining control. She grabbed at the wheel. He
lifted his left arm and struck her back-handed, in the
face. But this action was fatal. The junction was there
beside him and his left hand was off the wheel, the

car travelling much too fast. He tried to grab it round at the same time stamping on the brakes. With tyres squealing the car left the main road, bumped on to the grass verge and went skidding down the steep slope to the river, totally out of control and still moving fast.

When Mrs. Wood began to scream, Belinda, who had lain on the back seat half-stunned, shot up into a sitting position and realized at once that help was at hand though it might fail of its purpose. All her natural energy returned at the sight of the road block and the figures manning it. When the car began to spin towards the water she kept her head. She wound down the window nearest to her and reaching up turned on the inside lights of the car just as it toppled forward and plunged into the river, throwing up a cloud of spray.

The men on the bank saw the three figures suddenly illuminated. Hugh recognized Belinda and was out of his coat and shoes and into the water before the car was quite submerged. The lights were still on, showing its position. Hugh reached it and was about to swim down when a head surfaced beside him.

'Darling!' Belinda gasped. 'How on earth did *you* get here?'

It was such a silly question at that particular moment that they both laughed and swallowed water and choked. Then they swam to the bank and were helped out.

The river seemed to be full of splashing figures as three or four of the police tried to rescue the two left in the car. They found Mrs. Wood and brought her out and began artificial respiration. Mr. Burt was not in the car. At any rate they could not find him there in spite of repeated dives and when they raised the car at dawn it was empty. They did find him in the end, held fast in the reeds where Mavis had lain, where the current swept along the bank as the river narrowed to the bridge. Perhaps he had been drowned in the car and washed out when the rescuers managed to open the doors. Perhaps he had scrambled out as Belinda had done and thought he could swim away from his pursuers, but failed when the reeds caught his legs and arms and held him. Nobody much cared about the manner of his death. He had drowned evading arrest, after his crimes had been clearly proved.

Mrs. Wood's breathing was restored on the river bank, but she had not regained consciousness when the ambulance came to pick her up.

* * *

At Drews Cottage an ambulance and a police car arrived about five minutes after Mr. Burt's hired car had fallen into the river. They found an open door and a lighted house with an unconscious man alone in it.

The police car, which had brought Inspector Carfax himself to the cottage, stayed there as his temporary radio headquarters while Sir John was transferred to the ambulance and driven rapidly away to the hospital.

So when the Facel Vega arrived and Warrington-Reeve escorted two dripping figures indoors Carfax was able to give them the reassurance they wanted.

'He'll be all right, Miss Tollet,' he said. 'Quite all right. He's still asleep, but he was a good colour and breathing naturally.'

'How d'you know?' she demanded. 'You aren't a doctor. I heard them. They said – anyway, it meant they'd given him something to kill him and make it look like suicide. They thought he was dying. So did I. That's why I daren't wait till they'd gone before I phoned.'

'Very plucky action, miss,' Carfax congratulated her. 'I'm sure you needn't worry. Have a look at this.'

He led her to the fireplace and showed her the basket where logs for the fire were stacked.

'See all that wet?' he said. 'Coffee. He managed to get rid of the best part of his dose, I reckon, when he cottoned on to what they were up to.'

'But he didn't move!' Belinda cried, still unconvinced. 'His eyes were shut and he didn't move or open them even when he must have heard my voice ringing up.'

'If he had, the pair of you might not be alive now,' Carfax told her. 'But I think he had taken enough to put him to sleep, though not enough to do him any harm.'

Warrington-Reeve broke in.

'Belinda, you incredibly obstinate girl, stop standing there ruining your uncle's best carpet and go and have a hot bath this instant! If *you* don't mind getting pneumonia yourself you might think of Hugh, who has to wait till you've finished before he can bath in his turn.'

'He's right, darling,' Hugh said, through chattering teeth. 'Scram!'

When Belinda, suddenly restored to sanity, had gone upstairs, Hugh took off his own soaking clothes and wrapped himself in a rug Warrington-Reeve brought in from the Facel Vega. Inspector Carfax went out to his car to get into radio communication with the bridge and the other road blocks. The search for Burt was abandoned until daylight returned. He was not in the car, so that too could wait.

Superintendent Mitchell joined the party at Drews Cottage. He was about to leave for London in his second car but he wanted to explain one or two points to Warrington-Reeve.

'Sorry to upset your ingenious theories,' he said, 'but we know now that Burt was responsible for both murders. Ditchling was double-crossing him with Mavis's help. Burt realized this and struck back. He and Mrs. Wood must have met Ditchling in the woods just after he left the cottage. He must have gone that way to avoid meeting them in the road, but they anticipated this. There was no reason why he should be afraid of meeting Mr. Mellanby, was there? It was going to take him longer, but he was afraid of Burt, and rightly so. He gave the film to Mavis in the wood, to be on the safe side. Sir John must have refused to play at that stage, but we shall know more exactly when we are able to ask him about this interview. Anyway, Janet knows it was on this day that Mavis threw in her lot completely with Ditchling, though she didn't get any details. I'm sure Mrs. Wood was there with Burt and they kept Ditchling away from the bungalow until Mr. Mellanby had gone finally and then took him, ostensibly to argue it out, but really to give him a lethal dose of his usual drug. Later that night they must have driven past the cottage and put him in Sir John's car.'

'Why? Why not tip him in the river like Mavis?'

'Because they wanted him found in London, not in Southfield. Len Smithson – know who I mean? O.K. Len had orders to take the Jag. It was this that finally cleared Sir John, to my mind. This and finding out that Mrs. Wood, Mrs. Dorothy Wood, had worked in the same firm as Burt, whose real name was Simpkins.'

Warrington-Reeve nodded.

'This explains why Mrs. Wood arrived early that evening. She was already in the neighbourhood. Burt had only to drive her to the station, where she could go on to the platform and come off at the time a train from London arrived. She was too good an organizer not to have a ticket ready. She then took a taxi to the cottage while Burt drove off home.'

'That's right.'

'Those coincidences of yours,' Warrington-Reeve went on. 'I never liked them, either. Particularly the Jag. But Mrs. Wood as partner – well, that straightens it all out, doesn't it?'

'She was in Switzerland, though,' Hugh said, puzzled. 'How could she have helped with Mavis's death?'

'She wasn't. She came back on the next flight after Sir John. When Mavis went up to London to try to see him and sell him a print of the photo for her own benefit Burt and Mrs. Wood must have intercepted the girl as she left the flats. The caretaker said she wasn't there more than a quarter of an hour. He saw her leave.'

'The Jag,' Hugh said. 'If this Len was told to steal it as you said, and told Belinda was going to fetch it, what did he do with it between eight and nine? Or didn't he really leave the airport at nine?'

'I think he stayed in the airport,' Mitchell said. 'He'll make up a different story every time, so there isn't much point in asking him. He had to move it, but he could have taken it to a different car park.'

'But suppose Belinda had got there at eight and found it missing? She'd have made a fuss, after looking about for a bit and then what?'

'He had to risk that, being picked up, I mean, either at the airport or on the road. Burt had given his orders and however much Len disliked them he'd carry them out. Burt paid him very well. As it was he got away with it, until he had the puncture.'

'Burt wouldn't have cared if Len had been picked up with a body in the boot,' said Warrington-Reeve. 'Especially that of a double-crossing spiv like Ditchling.'

'Exactly. Len had something against Ditchling. Burt wouldn't have been incriminated, personally.'

'Then when they got hold of Mavis they drugged her and took her down to the river here, I suppose?' Hugh said.

'Must have.'

'Why did Mavis say Burt was to have the negative if she was double-crossing him? Why didn't she tell him where it was that night? It would have saved her life.'

'Obstinate and greedy. Still hoped Sir John would pay up in time. But ready to hand over to Burt if he proved too awkward. Unluckily for her she didn't recognize what he was doing until too late.'

'Nice people, all of them,' said Hugh.

'Particularly Mrs. Wood,' Warrington-Reeve added. 'I must say I had doubts about her when she tried to accuse Sir John of improper behaviour and got so emotional over it. Not in character.'

'No,' said Hugh. 'If it'd been genuine, she'd have given her notice without saying a word and walked out.'

Mitchell nodded.

'I wasn't altogether convinced by her act, myself,' he said.

He went to the telephone and called the hospital. It was a brief call. He went back to the now glowing fire.

'She died in the ambulance on the way in,' he said.

'Thank God for that!' Hugh murmured. He began to shiver again and drew the rug closer about his body.

'So we shall never know,' Warrington-Reeve said, slowly, 'why she took up with a man like Burt.'

'Kindred spirits, I think,' Mitchell said, briskly. 'She was a good secretary, orderly, neat, plenty of initiative. No outlet. Bored. Burt much the same. First-class organizer. Patient, careful, good on detail. Ought to have stuck to his snatch jobs. But they made a good pair. She was Mrs. Stott, too.'

'Yes, you told us.'

'Funny how one-track-minded they all are. She took a big risk trying to plant vice on Sir John.'

Belinda, coming down after her bath, wearing Sir John's pyjamas and dressing-gown, heard this last remark. But the superintendent had gone. She had to appeal for enlightenment to Warrington-Reeve, while Hugh, tripping over the fringe of the rug, stumbled upstairs in his turn.

*   *   *

The three of them spent the night at the cottage. In the morning Warrington-Reeve drove them to South-field Hospital, leaving them to make their own way to Sir John's bedside.

He was looking remarkably well. With modern treatment his fairly heavy dose of drug had been counteracted quickly. He had woken feeling only a

little muzzy, at his usual time, astonished to find himself in a hospital bed but quite capable of understanding what had brought him there. Carfax had called to
give him a full account of the whole case.

Belinda kissed him tenderly, while Hugh stood by
murmuring congratulations. Sir John kept his niece's
hand in his.

'So you were the only one, Linda, who refused to
believe unspeakable things of your uncle.'

Hugh reddened but could not deny the charge.

'It's curious,' Sir John went on. 'In Victorian, even
Edwardian days respectable people of some standing
were never suspected of indulging in the more purple
vices. Now everyone seems to expect it of them. In fact,
it is becoming quite dubious for two people of the same
sex to share a flat and as for platonic friendship – quite
impossible – if not unhealthy.'

'People always have thought the worst,' Belinda
said. 'Only they haven't always said it so loudly. I
expect that's the only difference.' She smiled at her
uncle and said, 'You did give us rather a test, didn't
you? Those hired cars and visits from little girls at
your flat.'

'Those,' answered Sir John, calmly, 'were children
from various youth clubs I'm interested in. I hired cars
because I attended those clubs as plain Mr. Drewson. I
didn't want displays laid on for my benefit; I wanted to
see what really went on at them. Hence the type of
car I used was not likely to attract attention. Any other
question?'

'Just one,' Hugh said. 'When they got Burt's car up
this morning, they found—'

'My money,' said Sir John, as calmly as ever. 'Oh
yes, I paid the crooks. I would have gone on paying
them. I could afford the money, but not the scandal.
A simple calculation, and not really incriminating. Or
do you think it must be?'

'Of course he doesn't,' Belinda said, indignantly. 'He
knows if he did I'd never marry him.'

Hugh put an arm round her. Sir John smiled at them both.

'I should congratulate you both, then,' he said. 'I'm delighted.'

Belinda kissed him again. Hugh murmured thanks but said no more. He was remembering that according to Mrs. Wood Sir John had said that scarf belonged to Belinda and he would give it back to her. Was this another of Mrs. Wood's lies, or—? Those hired cars. The Vanguard had stood at the flats in London all night, but had there been another car hired as well? Had Sir John gone out a little later than Mavis and the caretaker had not seen him? Had Len been told about the Jag simply because it was a good car to use for the raid? Had Burt really met Jeremy in the woods?

Hugh gave up. The police were satisfied; the criminals were dead and could not be brought to justice. Sir John, however formidable, however ruthless, was Linda's uncle; not, for him, any longer a subject for speculation. Besides, where could Sir John have got all those drugs? And the attempt on him, so much in keeping with the other murders. Besides again, he was convinced the old man was not a pervert. A murderer? He was ready to bury his doubt. This time he would take Warrington-Reeve's advice and keep at least one secret from his wife.

'You're looking very worried, darling,' Belinda said, leaning her head against his shoulder. 'Sorry you proposed to me?'

He forced a laugh.

'Actually I was thinking what a bore it would be for Sir John having to find a new secretary.'

'He mustn't get one through an advertisement, anyway,' said Belinda.

Sir John gave Hugh a keen look.

'She had such excellent references,' he said. 'But people are not always what they seem. Are they, Hugh?'